MW00911550

MYSTERY
IN MIAMI
BEACH

A Vivi Hartman Adventure

MYSTERY IN MIAMI BEACH

Harriet K. Feder

 Lerner Publications Company ■ Minneapolis

Library of Congress Cataloging-in-Publication Data

Feder, Harriet K.
    Mystery in Miami Beach : a Vivi Hartman adventure / Harriet K. Feder.
        p.   cm.
    Summary: While spending winter break with her grandmother in Miami Beach, freshman Vivi Hartman stumbles upon danger, Nazi hunters, and an old mystery involving the escape of the Jews from Germany just before World War II.
    ISBN 0-8225-0733-1 (lib. bdg.)
    [1. Jews—Fiction. 2. Miami Beach (Fla.)—Fiction 3. Mystery and detective stories.] I. Title.
PZ7.F2995My 1992
[Fic]—dc20   91-38735
                                                         CIP
                                                          AC

Manufactured in the United States of America

1 2 3 4 5 6 7 8 9 10 01 00 99 98 97 96 95 94 93 92

To Herb, for patience, reassurance,
and being there

I am deeply indebted to the Wednesday Night Workshop for their encouragement and critique of my manuscript, to Edith Cohen, Melvin Davidson, Chaim Kahn, and Dr. Sol Messinger for the invaluable sharing of their experiences, to Donna Prentiss for her helpful observations, to Sara Bossert, Millie Niss, Amy Shea, and Kelly Suckow, the young people who read this book in process, and most gratefully to my editor, Martha Brennecke, who saw its possibilities and helped make it all come together.

1

The plane had sat on the Buffalo airport tarmac for over an hour and we hadn't moved a single inch. Some of the passengers slept. Others walked around. I bit off the last of my nails and reached for my book, Shakespeare's *Troilus and Cressida*. I hadn't even looked at it yet, and we were having a test on it our first day back to school. I'd just started reading the play when a flight attendant asked if I wanted a magazine. The cover was a lot more tempting than *Troilus and Cressida*, but I resisted. The attendant didn't give up. He pointed to a newspaper. "How about a Miami *Herald*?" The thick, black headline glared at me: "MIAMI BEACH RESIDENTS STILL TERRORIZED."

Miami Beach? That was where I was headed, to visit my gram for winter break. I pounced on the paper, mumbling a hurried "thanks."

> **Miami Beach** An Israeli tourist has become the second senior citizen in two weeks to be beaten by a teen-age gang near the Harborfront Hall condominium. Erica Steinhardt is in critical condition after being attacked Thursday afternoon. . . . Miami Beach Police Chief A. R. Smith believes that the crimes are drug related. "These kids are so well organized," added Smith, "that we suspect there is an adult in charge. Give up your purse, not your life," he said.

My hands were shaking so hard I nearly dropped the paper. Erica Steinhardt! That was Gram's friend! Harborfront Hall was my grandmother's condo. I remembered our phone conversation of last week.

"Vivi darling, are you okay? I don't like the way you sound. Have you been working too hard in school? Will the world come to an end if you don't get an *A* in every subject?"

I'd sighed and told her I felt great, being careful not to sniffle.

"Great, huh? Sounds like you could use some Florida sun. Promise me you'll come?"

I promised.

"But Vivi."

"Yes?"

Gram hesitated. "You'll have to sleep in the den, darling. My friend Erica is visiting."

I ran the name through my head. It was one I didn't know. "Who's she?"

"Erica Steinhardt. You don't remember her? She lives in Israel now. She's just—visiting for a while."

I shrugged it off. So what was the big deal?

"You'll get the junk off the sofa bed?"

"The den will be so neat, Vivi dear, you won't recognize it."

I smiled. That would be a miracle.

"Promise you won't mind about the room?"

"Sure."

"And Vivi?"

"Yes, Gram?"

"Promise me you won't bring the dog. Last time they nearly threw me out of the building."

Before I hung up, I'd promised that too.

"A promise is a promise," my father had said, dropping five silver dollars into my hand. "Happy Hanukkah!" It was the same gift he gives me every year. Dad was a few days early this time, but who was counting?

I glared at him. It was all his fault that I had to go to Florida. Not that I didn't love Gram, but this was winter break, and Bob McKnight, the coolest-looking guy at South High, had asked me to be his date for the Snowball.

Bob McKnight! All six feet of him. I'd be the envy of the whole freshman class. All he had to do was stand beside me to make my five-foot-six-inch body seem petite. I closed my eyes and saw us gliding across the gym. Me in the orange synthetic silk formal from Hong Kong and those weird Italian patent leather pumps my mother had sent from Milan two years ago. In a daze, I wondered if they'd still fit. I saw Bob's sun-streaked hair against my ratty brown curls as he bent to whisper something in my ear.

Bob had moved to town just this fall. "This Honors Algebra?" he'd asked me, and I knew by his accent he'd come from Maine. I'm good at detecting things like that. Bob himself never said where he was from. He never said much of anything. We were always getting stuck for something to talk about. But who needed conversation when you looked so good together?

It was my best friend, Rachael, who'd sprung me back to reality.

"Great!" she said, dumping her books into our locker like it was any other ordinary day. "Only tell me something, Goody Two Shoes. You're always so scared of getting in trouble with Daddy, how will you hit the rabbi with Bob McKnight?"

"Very carefully," I answered.

All the way home on the bus, I made up speeches for Dad. But I might as well have sat and done my homework for all the good my speeches did.

Dad never even looked up from his desk. "A non-Jewish boy? It's out of the question." He turned a page of his book and wrote something in the margin. I almost screamed but was saved by my dog's bark. I went to the back door, opened it for Farfel, and hugged him, wiping my wet cheek against his fur. I needed his softness, but he wiggled out of my arms and ran to Dad.

"Farfel, shev!" my father commanded. The dog sat down at Dad's feet obediently and was rewarded with a biscuit. My father had never bribed me, I thought. I had to learn Hebrew for nothing. Dad rubbed Farfel's tummy. But then he was all business, using the tone of voice that he usually saved for funerals.

"The quicker you tell the boy no, the better. Call him tonight. It's not right to leave a kid hanging." He handed me the clean white handkerchief he always carried for emergencies. "And turn off the waterfalls, please. You're already a bat mitzvah, old enough to do what you know is right. Any other problems?"

Problems? I collapsed in the big leather "troubled souls" chair, picked up my dog, and buried my face against him. How could I tell Dad that the biggest problem I had was having a hardheaded, hardhearted rabbi for a father?

"But what can I say to Bob?" I moaned.

Dad turned back to his massive oak desk. "The truth, of course! Just say that I won't allow it." He reached for his thick black book and put on his stupid half-moon glasses. "That kind of business can lead to intermarriage."

Marriage? It was crazy. Bob and I had never even kissed. Not once had he marked up my locker like some of the freshman boys did when they liked a girl. For that matter, no one else had either. To the Jewish boys around, I could have been a stone statue on display in some old museum with "Do Not Touch" engraved on my forehead. Who would have the guts to party with the rabbi's daughter and then face him in Hebrew School the next day? But did Dad ever think about that? Of course not.

He put down the book and finished with a final flourish. "Marriage is hard enough these days even without religious differences."

He had this funny look he gets sometimes when he's thinking about my mother. He smiled, trying to mask it. Too late. Next June would make five years since the divorce. Mom had got her job teaching languages in Paris and, except for the summers, Dad had got me.

I swallowed the lump in my throat and wondered if things would be different if my mother were still around. I wondered if she would have backed me against my father. Then I wondered why I was wasting my time wondering. Mom wasn't here and nothing would change that. Even if she'd wanted to, she couldn't fight Dad from France. And she couldn't help me explain to the beautiful Bob

McKnight why I couldn't be his date for the Snowball either.

I'd put off telling him until Thursday after school, in the parking lot. I wish I could forget how he'd slammed his bike lock into his pack. "Your dad thinks I want to marry you?" he shouted. "I'm only fourteen! I asked you to a dance, not to our wedding!" It was the longest speech I'd ever heard him make. I hid my face in my scarf, convinced that everyone else had heard him too.

That night at dinner I hardly ate at all and made sure that Dad noticed it.

"I put too much pepper in the veal roast again?" he asked. "Take a drink of water and eat it anyway. It will put some fat on your bones. Keep you warm up north."

"North?"

"Yes. I thought we'd drive up to Canada. Do some skiing over the break."

I ground my teeth. Dad knows I hate skiing. Well, not skiing exactly. It's the lift that terrifies me. If I could take a bus to the top of the hill I might love to ski. I helped myself to a piece of cake. "Not me!"

He smiled. "If you don't like north, it can be south. Miami Beach. It's about time you paid Gram a visit, havaree." He'd called me his friend, but he wasn't treating me like one. Without any further discussion, he excused himself, went to the phone, and called Gram.

Gram was his solution to the "Bob problem." He'd figured it all out with his pilpul, no doubt. Pilpul is an ancient system of logic used for studying biblical questions. Sort of an intellectual workout. My father's such a pro at it that he uses it for all kinds of problems. I tried to trace his mental acrobatics:

"One, I have to get Vivi far away from that boy. Two, she probably won't come skiing, being scared to death of heights. Three, she loves her grandmother and she wouldn't refuse to pay her a visit. Which leads to four, she should go to Miami. She's scared to death of flying, too. But she manages to do it when necessary."

The night before I left, Farfel dragged his tail as he does whenever he sees me pack. And Rachael emptied my closet, bugging me as usual about clothes.

"You have to take at least one dress," she said. "What if you meet a boy who wants to take you someplace cool?" She closed her eyes and hugged herself. "What you need is the elegance of silk." I closed my eyes too and winced at the words. They'd come straight out of one of her fashion magazines. Rachael's room is carpeted with them. I pulled the orange formal off a hanger and rolled it into a tight little ball. Rachael yelled, "You're murdering it!"

"Not to worry," I told her. "It's just something my mother picked up in Hong Kong. She swore it couldn't be creased."

16

"Yeah? Did you ever try it out?"

I shrugged. "I hate it. Never had it on my back. And to think, it's indestructible. Watch!" I stuffed the orange silk ball into an old sneaker, stuck the whole thing in my pack, and zipped it up. I was finished. But Rachael wasn't. She opened a bureau drawer.

"You mean you're not even taking these great cotton shorts your Mom had made in Egypt? Or the shoes she sent you from Italy? And what about this Irish cardigan?" I pulled the sweater out of her hands to get her off my case. Then she hugged me and said goodbye, and it was all I could do to keep from crying my eyes out.

It was practically the crack of dawn when Dad and I went to the temple. I sat in the pew he'd assigned me when Mom took off. Second row, center aisle, where he could always keep an eye on me. Above the doors of the ark, the ten golden commandments glowed like the sun over the sanctuary. Dad's pale scholar's face, fringed by the short auburn beard, leaned over the scrolls. In one strong hand he grasped the silver pointer, marking the words that made me feel warm and safe. In his other hand I felt my invisible leash. Once again I'd strained against it, but not too hard. It was almost as if I were scared to death it might break. Rachael was right. I was a Goody Two Shoes, and I sat there hating myself for it.

The congregation was chanting without concern

for keeping a single pace. And Dad, wrapped in his huge white prayer shawl, spoke only to God. He was oblivious of everyone else, even of the women who looked at him more than they looked at their prayer books. They acted as though my mother were dead with no chance of ever coming back. Rolling their eyes, hanging onto his arm. "Wonderful sermon, Pat." "Will I see you at the Anniversary Ball?" "Got a little problem. Mind if I drop by next week, Patrick? Thanks. You're a saint. Oops, I didn't mean that."

His name had always been a puzzle. "Patrick Isaac Hartman," a Jewish kid named for a priest who'd made bishop. Dad would never discuss it. And my grandmother always answered the same way. "It's a fine name. It belonged to a wonderful man. A lot of good people agreed on the naming." It sounded as if a committee had been at the brit.

My father ended the service with the old familiar conclusion: "He who blesses, bless those among us who are ill at home and in the hospital (Dad named them all). May they soon be strong again." Then he looked at me, smiled, and winked one deep blue eye. "May it be your will, O Lord, that you bless my daughter, Aviva, as she starts on her holiday journey. May you guide her footsteps to reach her destination in life, gladness, and peace. May you rescue her from the hand of every foe, ambush, bandit, and all manner of evil on earth."

The words of that ancient blessing spun around in my head as I sat on the plane clutching the crumpled newspaper. The story of the brutal attack on Erica danced before my eyes. Would Gram be next? I needed to be with her, touch her, make sure she was all right. What was wrong with this plane? Why were we sitting here with the doors still open? I tossed my Irish knit cardigan on the empty seat near the window and looked out. Who were we waiting for? Some VIP?

I worried that we'd never take off, and that I wouldn't get to see my grandmother alive. Then I worried that we would take off, and that the plane would never make it. My heart was doing a tap dance. I took a deep breath, put down the paper, and tried to concentrate on Shakespeare. The pen skidded in my sweaty hands as I wrote the name "Troilus" over and over in the margin. Minutes? Hours? How long had I been at it when I heard that voice in my ear?

"What about Cressida, eh?"

2

His inflection was Canadian, province of Ontario. Maybe he came from Toronto, only a couple of hours from Buffalo. My mother can keep all those high-style European clothes, but I owe her for my supersensitive ear. It definitely comes from her side of the family.

"That play's not bad," the boy said, "but not as good as the Henrys. Old Shakespeare really dug history." There was something about the sounds, an undertone I hadn't caught at first. It came from the Bronx, yet I doubted that he'd ever lived there. I underlined "Troilus" and glued my eyes to the edge of the kid's jeans. His sneakers were almost as cruddy as mine. Some VIP!

He threw his bag in the overhead compartment and squeezed in front of me, going for the empty window seat. When his back was turned toward me, I couldn't miss the gigantic patch on the back of his T-shirt—a bright red bird flying between his shoulders.

He was skinny and tall, taller even than Bob McKnight. I didn't dare to look at his face until he was sitting down, staring at a book through mammoth dark glasses that hid his eyes. He was gorgeous. I thought about Dad and sighed. With that jet black hair, olive complexion, and my kind of luck, this guy would turn out to be a Canadian Eskimo. The plane started to taxi and he looked up. I buried my face in *Troilus and Cressida*.

"Going to Miami, eh?"

The Ontario lilt was pure music, but I couldn't enjoy it. I stared straight ahead, petrified of taking off. Sure I was going to Miami—if I lived to get there. I closed my eyes. It wouldn't hurt to pray.

"That's where I'm going," the kid said. "My uncle runs a fishing boat down there. I help him out on every school vacation." When I still didn't answer, he stuck his nose back in his book.

As I finished my prayer, an attendant came to the aisle. She held an oxygen mask and showed me how it worked. A voice on the intercom told me what to do in case we crashed. If it happened over the ocean, my seat would become a raft. On land, the wing of the plane could be a slide. "Please locate the nearest emergency exit," the voice told me. It was good advice but I didn't take it. I stared straight ahead while we took off, hugging the arm-rests as if I were going to take them with me to the grim end. A half hour later, when the attendant brought my lunch, I could barely unlock my hands.

"Aviva Hartman? You ordered a kosher meal?" She held out a foil-covered package, but I was too nervous to take it. The kid on my right took it for me.

"Your name is 'Hartman,' eh? I read a book once by a Rabbi Hartman. I remember it 'cause his first name was so weird. Patrick, or something." He unhinged my table, and I prayed he didn't see me wince. "You're lucky," he said. "They haven't even started serving us peasants yet."

He was right. I was lucky. I was still alive. I'd been too uptight to eat breakfast and was starving. The package smelled like spaghetti and meatballs. Kosher spaghetti and meatballs. What a jackpot! I carefully turned one foil corner back.

"It's hot. Let me help you," the boy said. Crash! My meal was on the floor. I stared at it in horror. Goopy red strands of spaghetti lay twisted around squashed meatballs, turning the carpet into a Persian rug. My broccoli was a still life on a back-ground of creamy white dressing. The pungent scent of oregano was everywhere.

The kid took off his glasses and wiped away some of the goop.

"Gosh, I'm sorry," he said. I knew he wasn't lying. I could tell by his eyes, hazel with gorgeous gold flecks. The attendant looked sorry too. "There isn't another kosher meal on board," she said. "We carry the exact number ordered."

"What about vegetarian?" It seemed like my only hope.

She shook her head. "It's the same. Can I get you some tomato juice? A glass of milk perhaps? We usually have extra for the children."

"No, thanks."

"How about a candy bar?" the kid asked me. Candy? My mouth started to water just thinking about it. He reached into his pocket. Chocolate, wouldn't you know! I shook my head. Chocolate always made my face break out.

"Listen," he said, holding out his hand, "we can still be friends, eh? I'm Mike. Micah Abramson." I liked his smile. I like the sound of his name, too. Micah! An Old Testament name if I ever heard one. Even my father couldn't find fault with that.

"I'm from Canada," he volunteered.

I moved a little closer. "Ontario by way of the Bronx, right?"

The smile disappeared. "Afraid not." He turned back to his book, like a turtle escaping into its shell. My first Jewish boy and I'd blown it already with my prying. What to do? Try singing "O Canada?" I could hum it but I didn't know the words.

"That book any good?" I asked.

"This?" He shrugged. "It's a history of World War II. Over five hundred pages. I'll be lucky to get through it by fifth year."

"Fifth?"

He nodded. "You Americans are always moaning about four years of high school. But in Ontario we have one more than you. Two down and three to go before college. What a drag."

Once Mike and I got started we seemed to have plenty to talk about. I put on hold my fear of heights, my worry over Gram, and the brutal attack on Erica, while we blabbed about hockey, sitcoms, and soccer. There were only two topics I made sure to avoid: Micah Abramson's Bronx connection and my connection to Rabbi Patrick Hartman.

3

The Greater Miami airport was wall-to-wall people. I pushed through the crowd, toward the special place outside where my grandmother was supposed to be waiting.

"Stop," Mike said, pulling my arm. "I never got your phone number." He was holding a pen and a small scrap of paper against his history book.

"Phone number?" Oh my God, what was Gram's phone number? I knew I'd once had it in my head. "Five-five-five, one-two-nine-nine," I yelled above the roar of the crowd.

"Two nines?"

I turned to answer but Mike wasn't around. A second later I saw him lying on the ground, a giant fullback type on top of him. Book, pen, and paper had landed in various places nearby. Mike grabbed his book. The man grabbed Mike and pulled him to his feet. His square jaw was tight as he spoke. "Mind what I told you, eh wot?" He sounded as if he had just stepped off a plane from England. As he moved away, I saw the front of his pullover. The bright red patch was a bird—the same as the one on the back of Mike's T-shirt. A new style in men's tropical fashions? Or was this some kind of fraternity?

I picked up the scrap of paper that had landed at my feet and tried to hand it to Mike. It was futile. The crowd kept moving us farther and farther apart. Soon, all that was left of our romance was a tiny scrap of paper with part of Gram's phone number on it. I stuck it in my pocket and made my way outside to look for Gram, slamming into a fat, brassy blond.

"Sorry," I said, feeling guilty. It wasn't her fault that I'd just lost Mike forever.

It had to be a hundred degrees in the shade and I was schlepping the wool cardigan that my mother had bought me at the duty-free shop in Shannon. We'd been on our way from Paris to Alaska for her research on Eskimo languages. The mere thought of going to Alaska had turned my lips blue.

"It's the perfect thing," Mom had said about the sweater.

And it was—for Alaska. But it wasn't exactly the

"thing" for Florida. Why had I let Rachael talk me into bringing it? I shifted the sweater to my other arm and blinked against the sun. Then I opened my eyes again. Miracle of miracles, who should I see but Mike?

He was down at the far end of the walk, talking to a girl. My heart fell into my shoes at the sight of her. A slim, sleek girl with straight black hair falling to her shoulders. Her face was half-hidden by a gigantic straw hat. Aside from the hat, the wildest thing about her was her shoes: slingbacks with skinny four-inch heels. I would have bet they were those chic Bruno Magli's I'd seen in Rachael's fashion magazines.

I swung my Irish knit cardigan in front of my cruddy jeans and pushed one dirty sneaker behind the other. Then I saw a man walking toward the two of them, holding a large red setter on a leash. The man hugged Mike, then kissed the girl long and hard. I took my foot out of storage and lifted the cardigan. The uncle with the boat? His feet were stuck into double-strap sandals. His legs were bare to the hems of his knee-length cutoffs. With his sun-bleached hair, darkly tanned face, and wrinkled cotton shirt, he looked like he spent a lot of time on the water.

"Hey, Mike," I called, walking toward them.

Mike turned. "Hey, Vivi. That you?" The girl gave me an icy stare. But the man smiled at me and bent to scratch his dog behind the ear. Then, all of a sudden, the dog broke loose and bolted.

The man gave Mike a shove. "Go get him!" Mike took off like a rocket. I followed as fast as I could. A few yards ahead, the crowd had parted where Mike stood yelling at the dog. The animal was running around in circles, its leather leash whipping the ground. Each time it passed him, Mike made a grab for it but lost. At last, with a running tackle, he brought the hound down. The mob moved in again and closed the gap. I jumped, waved, and yelled at Mike, but it was no use.

A van pulled up to the curb, its panels ablaze with pictures of fish and the words "NOAH'S ARK / FOR THE BEST CATCH IN TOWN—INDI-VIDUAL RATES AND GROUP CHARTERS." A door slid open and the dog jumped inside. Mike stood at the curb, his eyes searching for a moment. Then he ducked and climbed in the van.

I was tired, my head pounded, I felt sick to my stomach, and I was beginning to get awful cramps. When I finally found my grandmother I melted into her arms.

"You look awful," Gram said. "You're as pale as a ghost."

I shrugged. "It's the crowds and the temperature, and I think I'm getting my period besides."

"Shush, Vivi." Gram looked around. "That Hasid over there nearly heard you. They're not supposed to hear things like that."

I looked at the Hasid in his long black coat. A

dark corkscrew side curl hung in front of each ear, below the brim of his fur-trimmed hat. He spun around, showing me his back. Hasids weren't supposed to look at women—unless, of course, they were very close relations. So why did I have the feeling he'd been standing there staring at me?

"How can he stand the heat dressed like that?" I asked Gram.

She smiled. "When you're that religious, God helps you bear everything."

I sighed and took a better look at my grandmother, wondering if I should ask about Erica.

"You okay, Gram?"

Her bright brown eyes twinkled out of the depths of her folded skin. "Terrific! Tessie Terrific they call me down here." She tapped her umbrella on the concrete walk for emphasis. It was a big black thing, and pretty ugly.

"What's that for?" I asked.

"This? For the sun. It's wonderful for sudden rainstorms, too."

"For the sun? Boy, could I use that!" I reached for the umbrella.

She pulled it away. "Don't touch it, Vivi! Ever! You hear?"

I jumped back.

"It was a gift from a friend," she said more softly. "I promised I'd take good care of it."

"You mean Erica?" I managed.

Gram didn't answer. She touched my cheek.

"Come here and let me look at you. You're so skinny it's a wonder I could find you in this mob."

She hugged me and I gagged at the stench of turpentine. As long as I'd known her Gram had been a worrier, but she'd only started to smell after Grandpa died. That's when she took up painting again and went at it as if she were making up for lost time. Splotches of dried paint were sprinkled all over her smock as if she'd come to the airport straight from the easel. She looked older than the last time I'd seen her.

"Your baggage should be here by now," she said. "Let's go in and collect it."

"What's to collect?" I pointed to my backpack. "It's right here."

"That's all you brought?" Gram stepped back to see me better. Her inspection started at my forehead and traveled to the bottoms of my jeans, with a brief stop at my right thigh where a blob of dried spaghetti sauce lingered.

"My son doesn't only starve you. He doesn't take time to clothe you either," she said. "That's what becomes of a child with no woman around."

I bit my lip and moved to a safer topic. "Speaking of starving, how about lunch? I sort of lost mine on the plane."

"You threw up again?"

"Not exactly." I took her arm and pointed her toward the parking lot. But Gram wasn't giving up.

"That father of yours should be thinking about

30

getting married again. It's not good for a man to be alone. Tell me the truth, Vivi. Is there anybody in the picture yet?"

I thought of the single women in Dad's congregation, all no doubt asking for him in their prayers.

"Sure, Gram," I said, "they're standing in line. But if I were you, I wouldn't call the caterers yet."

In the parking lot, she warned me about the cracks in the asphalt. "Watch out where you walk. It's easy to break a leg around here." In the car, she warned me about the seat belt. "Make sure to pull it tight. Accidents kill more people than cancer."

Gram's old bus lurched into gear. If not for the seat belt, I would have flown to the floor just like her big ugly umbrella. I tried to pick it up. Her hand grabbed mine and squeezed it like a vise.

"Remember what I told you about this," she said, slowing the car to a crawl and stopping in a toll booth line. I gave up, slumped in my seat, and stared out the window.

A blood red sports car moved up in the adjacent line. Gram paid the toll and hung a right. The sports car fell in behind us. We took the next left, then stopped for a light. I glanced back. The car was still on our tail. The driver was looking in the mirror, holding a tissue to her mouth. Her dark hair fell around her shoulders. Her eyes and nose were almost completely hidden under her huge straw hat.

I swung around and stared straight ahead at the road. I didn't have to see any more. I knew that the shoe on the pedal was a Bruno Magli slingback, and I'd bet it had a four-inch heel. But why was she following me? Why had she shot me that icy stare at the airport? Jealousy? Was she secretly in love with Mike? I sat up. Of course! Behind the uncle's back, she and Mike were having a secret affair.

But even with my wild imagination that was ridiculous. Mike was a nice, ordinary kid from Toronto, not some sneaky Romeo. Or was he? Why did he almost flip when I mentioned the Bronx? And what was the story with the big red bird? Mike was from Canada. But the Englishman had a bird patch too. Did any of it compute with what had happened to Erica? Oh, God, had I stumbled onto some kind of international drug ring?

I wiped the sweat off my forehead and pictured Rachael, on the late-night news, tearfully telling the reporter we'd been best friends. I saw my father standing over my grave. "And she'd never been kissed by a boy," he said, tossing a handful of dirt into the hole. Oh, Dad, I thought, I finally met someone cool and Jewish, and we have so much to talk about. But is he worth my life? With Bob Mc-Knight all I had to do was dance.

4

"Don't look around, but someone's following us, Gram," I whispered. "It's that girl in the red sports car. Think you could go a little faster and try to lose her?"

Gram glanced at me and then in the mirror. "That woman in the hat? Vivi dear, you've been watching too much TV."

"Woman?" I looked again. She was a bit older than I'd thought. We crawled a few miles, then made a sharp left into a private lot, almost dragging down a sign that said "Goldstein's."

"First thing on our list is lunch," Gram said. "Put some flesh on your bones." If I'd been smart I would have asked what was second. But I wasn't, and besides, I was too uptight.

Gram was right, I thought. I had been watching a lot of weekend TV. I'd had to do something while everyone else was partying. But if the person in the coupe wasn't following us, why was she turning into Goldstein's lot this minute? She double-parked the coupe, sprang through the restaurant door, and was back in her car before Gram had crawled into the last shaded parking space.

"What are you waiting for?" Gram said. "I thought you were hungry."

I dragged myself out of the car. No one would attack a person here, in sight of all these people, would they? It wasn't a bad guess. The dark-haired woman never glanced our way.

Gram looked at the retreating sports car and then at me. "With your imagination," she said, "you should sit down and write a novel."

I'd been in Goldstein's with my grandmother a few times before. It's a special kind of deli. All of the waiters wear skullcaps, and the food's strictly kosher. I can eat nonstop without accidentally devouring pork or shellfish. In fact, the place is so kosher they not only have separate dishes for meat and dairy, they have separate dining rooms.

I headed for the spaghetti and meatballs department but Gram tugged at my arm. "Meat is the worst thing for the heart," she said. "If you stop eating it you'll feel like a new person." I didn't want to be a new person. I tried to tell that to Gram but she was already finding a table behind the "DAIRY—NO SMOKING" sign.

"Hello, Tessie. That's your granddaughter?" a woman called from a booth. A pair of wooden crutches leaned against the bench beside her.

Gram smiled. "Well, who else would it be, Sadie? She's some beauty, no?" Everyone should have a grandmother. You're always gorgeous in her eyes. What sane person would dare refute mine?

Gram poked my arm. "Say hello to Sadie from two floors down. You remember her, don't you?" I nodded toward the booth, sticking my hand in my pocket for a tissue to cover my red face. But what I pulled out was Mike's small scrap of paper. I hadn't noticed before that it was newsprint, and the first part of Gram's phone number was scrawled above a small classified ad. While Gram and her friend were talking, I read it:

Volunteers sought: Parties interested in helping to retrieve "mystery box," spotted last week by
captain of glass-bottom boat may
call 555-0893 or write to Noah,
Haulover Pier, M.B. 33141.

Noah! Like *Noah's Ark* on the van! Was Noah Mike's uncle? My pulse raced. Mike was staying with him and the number was right here. If only I could get up the nerve to call.

"What's that you have there?" my grandmother asked.

I handed her the paper. "Sounds like fun. I think I'll volunteer. It will give me something to do while you're painting."

"NO!" The diners nearby looked up at the shout. "I mean, it's too late," she whispered. "It's all over. This article's at least three weeks old."

"You mean they brought up the box?"

My grandmother didn't answer. She crumpled the scrap of paper and threw it on a busboy's tray, right into a bowl of leftover vegetable soup. It probably drowned before it ever hit the disposal. If only I hadn't found it at all, never got my hopes up again, I wouldn't have been so let down. My "waterfalls" threatened to tumble over the cliffs. I had as much of a chance now of finding Mike as of finding meatballs in the dairy section of Goldstein's.

"What are you going to have?" asked a waiter, coming up to our table.

"Nothing," I mumbled. "I'm eating my heart out." No one seemed to hear me.

"I'm waiting for Evan," said Gram, "the one who just started today." The waiter shrugged and left. Seconds later another waiter was at her side. He turned toward me, his back to Gram. Pretty rude, I thought, but Gram didn't seem to mind. She spoke up, ignoring the menu as if she knew it by heart. "I'll have herring, Evan," she said, "but leave off the cream sauce. It has more salt than the ocean.

Every time you eat it you commit suicide. And bring me a cup of coffee. Decaffeinated! Caffeine's just another killer."

"Well they'll never do *us* in, eh wot?" said the waiter. I stared at him. Another Englishman? One with a skullcap on his head? What were all these British doing in Florida? He was big-boned and tall just like the Englishman at the airport. But this one had a beard and he wasn't like any waiter I'd seen before. He never wrote down the order. Didn't even carry a pencil and pad.

"And what about you, love?" he asked me. My face became a ripe tomato.

"Bagel with cream cheese and lox," I whispered. "Coffee?"

"Don't be ridiculous!" my grandmother said. "She's only just past bat mitzvah." I would have hidden my face behind a menu but the waiter had already taken them away.

Even without a pen and pad, he did okay by lunch. But Gram played with her herring and still wasn't finished when Evan brought her decaf.

"Ready for your takeout, dearie?" he asked.

Gram sighed. "Yes. And maybe just a little something extra."

The waiter smiled. "A nice orange, perhaps?"

Gram's eyes lit up. But a second later they clouded over. "She has plenty of oranges at the hospital. The Harborfront Hall committee sent her a beautiful basket of fruit."

Hospital? I held my breath. They had to be talking about Erica. Gram looked at me and then at Evan, and I thought I saw him nod. Then he left and she turned to me. Her face was pale, her eyes were moist.

"Vivi dear, there's something I must tell you. It's about my good friend Erica. Something has happened. I don't know quite how to tell you. You mustn't be upset."

I reached out and took her hand. "I know, Gram. I read about it in the paper."

"The paper? Yes. Of course, the paper. I should have known." Gram wiped her eyes with a napkin. "We grew up together in the Bronx. She was Grandpa's first cousin and my best friend."

"Was? You mean she's—"

"No! Oh, no. At least not yet. It's just that I've hardly seen her since she moved to Israel. Such a beauty she was, and now—" Gram dug into her purse, took out a tissue, and blew her nose. "They took her to St. Francis Hospital. It's the closest one around."

"So that's the reason for the takeout?"

Gram nodded. "I bring her meals every day. She won't trust the meals at St. Francis even though they swear they'll feed her kosher."

Gram looked at her watch. "I'd drop you at the apartment but I'm already late, dear. Would you mind tagging along?"

"Of course not." I squeezed her hand and we sat

there not saying anything until Evan returned with the package.

"Tell Mr. Goldstein to put everything on my bill," Gram said.

The waiter smiled. "Don't you worry about the bill, love. Mr. Goldstein said it will all even out in the end. And don't forget this!" He handed Gram her umbrella, then smiled and pressed my hand, bowing so low I could see his skullcap. It was a deep blue like that of the other waiters. Only one thing was different. In the middle of the blue knit circle was a small red knit bird.

5

Every window was open, but the car was as hot as a sauna. We plodded along at thirty on the sixty-mile-an-hour highway. Horns bleated. Drivers slammed their fists against the windows of their air-conditioned cars. My grandmother waved to them and smiled. But the smile became a frown when I started asking about Erica.

"Who attacked her?"

Gram sighed. "Bunch of teenage hoodlums."

"Where did it happen? What was she doing going out alone?"

"It was right outside the supermarket. She'd only gone to get a loaf of bread. Enough already, Vivi. Look, we're at the hospital. You go get a visitor's pass while I park the car."

I got the pass and we took the visitors' elevator to the third floor. Halfway down the corridor of the west wing, Gram knocked at a door.

"Is that you, Tessie?" a weak voice called out.

"Of course it's me. Who did you expect, the queen of England?" Gram answered. I followed her into a darkened room where an elderly woman was sitting up in bed. In the half-light, the woman's eyes looked sunken. Her skin hung loose around her neck. Everything about her looked yellow—from her jaundiced face above the faded hospital gown to the few lifeless hairs that stuck out beneath the iodine-stained bandages on her head.

"Erica darling, look who I brought you," Gram said. The woman looked from my grandmother to me and a smile softened her face.

"Vivi! Little Vivi," she said in Hebrew. I wasn't little anymore, but I guess old images die hard.

"Don't you remember me?" she asked. "You don't remember the presents I used to bring you?" I guess it was the word "present" that blasted me back to my childhood. Suddenly I did remember. I recalled how she laughed. How she had called me in Hebrew "the pretty little girl." How she had brought toys and candy out of a big old trunk. She held out her arms now and I walked to the bed and hugged her.

My grandmother hung her umbrella on the back of a chair and sat down.

"Don't hang it there, Tessie, you'll forget it," Erica said, speaking English for the first time. Her accent had me stumped. It wasn't from the Bronx. It wasn't pure Israeli either. It wasn't anything I could pin down.

Gram held out the bag from the deli. "Here, take a whiff. It's pastrami on rye with sauerkraut on the side."

"From Myron's place?"

"Where else? Go ahead, take it. Evan packed it himself."

"Evan?" Erica took the bag, removed a sandwich, and unwrapped it. "What did Evan say?"

Gram shrugged. "Not to worry about the bills. Goldstein thinks it will all even out. And it will. You'll see. Now eat a little. We won't stay long. You need your rest."

Erica shivered. "Who can rest? That Hasid's face keeps coming back to me. That long black beard, those corkscrew curls, and the long black coat. I know he's the one. He was right there in the doorway with his eyes on those kids, directing them. Sadie saw him too. She was waiting for the rain to stop, standing under the awning between that man who just moved in, Mr. Johnson, and our friend with the—"

"Hush," Gram whispered, nodding toward me.

Erica sighed. She took a few bites of the sandwich then put the food on the nightstand and closed her eyes.

"Maybe she'll sleep," Gram said to me. "Let's go." She stood up and touched her lips to her friend's forehead.

"Don't forget the umbrella, Tessie," Erica whispered. "And be careful, havaree. Be careful, my friend."

The Harborfront Hall condominium is sixteen stories high, with a pool, hot tub, and shuffleboard court on the roof. Its sun-bleached brick walls curve around a marina on Biscayne Bay. It's only five blocks from the hospital, a ten-minute walk—twenty in a car with Gram driving.

"Who's this Hasid who has poor Erica scared to death?" I asked as we crept toward home.

Gram sighed. "Who knows? There's a political split in Israel between Hasids and everyone else, so a lot of Israelis see them as villains. But thinking a local Hasid is the boss of those teenage kids is crazy. Her brain must be confused from the concussion." It was Gram's longest speech on the subject so far. I hoped for even more, but that was all of it.

Why did I have the feeling there were things Gram didn't want me to know about? Why had she needed the waiter's okay to tell me about Erica? Why had she stopped Erica from talking in front of me? "Our friend with the—" That's all she'd let her say. What was the rest of it?

It wasn't until we got to my grandmother's street that I noticed the red sports car behind us. "Our

43

friend with the—" HAT! Of course! So she had been there too when Erica was mugged. And here she was still following us. Why was Gram protecting her? Or was she only trying to keep me from being scared?

Yes. That was it. It had to be. The woman with the hat wasn't following me at all. She was following Gram, and Gram didn't want me to know. Gram didn't want to worry me. But what could this woman want from my grandmother? All Gram owned besides her condo were her paintings.

Gram had studied art in New York City when she was young, but I'd never thought she was a great painter. Could it be that her pictures were really valuable? Most of them were hanging in her apartment. Had those kids mugged Erica for the key? An awful thought sent shivers down my spine. Paintings became more valuable after the artist was dead.

I felt my blood draining and prayed to God that Gram wouldn't notice how pale I'd become. Then I prayed I could keep my mouth shut and not let on to Gram that I knew. After that I prayed that God would hear my prayers and promised I'd protect my grandmother even with my life if necessary. I was laying it on a bit thick, but God knows me by now.

What a vacation this was so far. The only plus was meeting Mike. I knew he couldn't be part of whatever the woman with the straw hat had in mind. He probably hardly knew her, I told myself, and I felt miserable all over again about losing him.

Gram parked the car in the garage below the building and we rode a self-service elevator up to the lobby. From there we got one that went to her penthouse. It had to be after four because Pedro, the night-shift elevator operator, was on duty. He was wearing his usual starched gray uniform, with those black patent leather shoes that were shined so bright you could see your face in them. The way he said, "Buenas Tardes, señorita," as he touched his cap, always made me feel like I was the star of a late-night movie.

"How've you been, Pedro?" I asked. "Haven't seen you in ages." Pedro closed the door behind us and opened his mouth. It was as far as he got before Gram interrupted.

"Fine," she answered for him. Pedro just smiled and nodded. He was used to Gram's ways.

"I work a little for the señora on the side," he said. "Put all new locks on her door."

"Locks?" I turned to Gram. "But you had a good burglar alarm. It connected right up to the police station and alerted the cops right away. How can plain old locks compare to that?"

Pedro shrugged. "I try to tell her, but the señora say to change it."

"The police have enough to do these days," said Gram. "A person shouldn't bother them without reason." I bit my tongue to keep from exploding. Pedro sighed. He stopped the elevator at the private hall of the penthouse. Gram put her purse on the credenza and I waited while she fumbled with some keys. She picked out two with different-colored edges.

"You have to be careful to use the red one first," she explained, "and to open the bottom lock before the top one. It's two turns to the left and one to the right on the bottom lock. On the top, it's the other way around. Watch me carefully now." The lesson took forever. It was a good thing I didn't have to go to the bathroom.

What hits you first when you enter Gram's apartment is *A Field of Purple Asters,* the canvas that won her a scholarship to art school.

"It gave me life," Gram always said. I stood before it, startled one more time by the soft lavender blossoms on their tall willowy stems, the crystal droplets of moisture glinting in the sun. I tore myself away and looked around for other familiar pictures. That's when I saw the painting on the far wall.

It was an oil I'd never seen before—a building on a treeless hill, red brick and gray mortar walls surrounded by a concrete yard. It had to be a school, with all those kids in the yard. A small group stood in a circle, their arms around each other's shoulders, heads bowed as if in prayer. In the right-hand corner of the canvas was the title, *The Meeting,* and under that were the initials "T.K." I wasn't sure if I liked it or not. The style was different from the others.

"Who did this?" I asked Gram.

She smiled. "Who? I did, of course."

"But it isn't your style. And the last initial isn't yours either."

Gram laughed. "The 'K' is for 'Kovah,' my family name. This picture's more than fifty years old. I painted it back in high school. Had it stored away all these years."

"What made you drag it out now?"

Gram shrugged. "Erica insisted on it. For sentimental reasons," she added quickly. She gave me a little hug. "Anyway, I'm glad you got to see it since it will be yours someday."

"Mine?"

"Of course. They're all going to you. All of my paintings. It's already in my will."

I wormed out of her embrace. "Then I hope I never get them." Gram turned me around and made me face her.

"Listen, Vivi, death is a part of life. Coming to terms with death makes what you do with your life more important. Do you understand what I mean, my darling?"

I fastened my eyes on the carpet. "I'm not sure."

Gram kept hold of my arms. "One day we grow up. We realize our years are numbered. Yet there are so many things in this world we want to do. We have to make some very hard choices. Take your mother, for instance."

"My mother?"

"Yes." Gram's fingers were hurting my arms. "She did what she had to do even though it must have torn her to pieces. She's not coming back, Vivi. It's time you realized that. But you must try to find room in your heart for her anyway."

I tore out of Gram's arms. What right did she have to say that? Telling me what to do was one thing. But telling me what to feel was something else. She'd never done that before. Why now?

Why now? A moan started somewhere inside me and ended as a lump in my throat. Did Gram think she wouldn't have another chance? I reached for her, but she turned away and walked toward the kitchen. "Time to unpack," she said.

My backpack felt like a boulder as I dragged it automatically to the spare bedroom I called the "blue room." I'd stayed there on every visit and had forgotten it wasn't mine this trip. I touched the blue ruffled cover of forget-me-nots on the canopied bed and looked at the soft matching curtains at the windows. Blue used to be my favorite color and forget-me-nots were my favorite flower. Gram had fixed up the room just for me when I was eight. How could I break it to her that I was almost fourteen and into brown and hyacinths when she'd even made a forget-me-not cover for the rocking chair?

The rocking chair! Where was it? Something else was taking up its space. A trunk. Like the one I take to Europe every summer, only bigger. With a rush I realized it was Erica's.

I touched the peeling black paint and smelled the trunk's mustiness. It had to be ancient with all those deep scratches and old travel stickers. There were stickers from the Israeli airline El Al and a few from other airlines. Another worn yellow sticker had a picture of a ship on it. I could barely make out the name—*Queen Mary.*

Then a picture on the dark mahogany dresser caught my eye. A black-and-white photo in an old-fashioned, flowery frame: a man, a woman, a girl about my age, and a very small boy. The girl had dark hair and black, solemn eyes. The boy was fair with a serious set to his mouth. His little round face ended in a squared-off chin. I was looking at it when Gram came into the room.

Her voice was soft. "A sweet picture, isn't it? Erica, her parents, and her baby brother, Marc. Did you forget her things were in here, Vivi? Come, I tried to clean the den as best I could, but there might be a few odds and ends around."

I knew that meant the den was loaded with junk. I was right. The books in the floor-to-ceiling book-shelves seemed to have reproduced through the years. Assorted papers and books lay all over the place, just like in my father's study. It looks like a tornado lit down, I thought. Immediately I knew that was exactly what my mother would have said, and I hated myself for having thought it.

I grabbed the sneaker with the orange synthetic silk dress inside and threw it on the closet shelf.

That made me feel a lot better. Then, starting from the left, I put my red shirts, white shirts, and yellow shirts away. Hanging my clothes in any other order made me feel out of sync with the alphabet. I was folding some underwear when Gram put her head in the door.

"I'm going up to the roof," she said. "I'll be back by the time you're unpacked."

I slammed the drawer shut. "Wait! I'll go with you!" No way would she give me the slip. I'd promised God I'd protect her, hadn't I?

But Gram shook her head. "You'll stay right here, young lady. You've been dragging around since early this morning. What you need is a nice bath and a nap."

"I'm not a bit tired," I lied. "And I don't want a bath. I want a swim. I can't wait to get to the roof and jump into the pool." I closed my eyes, praying she'd believe me. That was my first big mistake.

"Why are you closing your eyes?" Gram asked. "Do you have a headache?" She felt my head. "At least there's no fever."

"Why should I have a fever? I'm not sick. You might as well face it, Gram. With all the muggings going on down here, you're not going anywhere without me!"

My grandmother smiled. "Oh, so that's it. You think I need a bodyguard because of what happened to Erica? Vivi dear, relax. Believe me, I won't be attacked on the roof." She laughed. "Except maybe by Sadie from two floors down. She can talk a person half to death." Gram opened a cupboard, got out some linens, and handed them to me. "I've got one of those newfangled plastic ice packs in the freezer," she said. "It's better for headaches than aspirin. Aspirin is poison for the system. Lie down for five minutes with the ice pack. When you wake up you'll feel like a new person." With that great advice, Gram was gone.

"O Lord," I whispered, "you know I tried. But I guess the roof is safe enough."

I finished unpacking and looked at the couch. What a mess! I scooped up an armful of papers and started to carry them to the desk. But something in the pile slipped out—a small blue card. As it landed on the floor, the card flipped open and I saw the Hebrew writing inside. My body began to tremble as I read it.

6

I held the card with clammy hands. The block letters blurred then came into focus again. First Gram's name, then below it the veiled Hebrew message:

"HAPPY HANUKKAH! IT'S YOUR TURN NOW." Beneath the words, a tiny red bird stared at me with beady black eyes. There was no signature.

The ringing of the phone tore me out of my stupor. I managed a shaky "Hello?"

"That you, Mother?"

"Dad!"

"Oh, it's you, Vivi. You're alive. I was beginning to wonder. You were supposed to ring me up hours ago when your plane arrived. You promised."

Dad, oh, Dad! I fought back the cry. "Sorry. Guess I forgot."

"Forgot? When I'm sitting here worrying? A promise is a promise, Vivi. Did you forget that, too? Speak up. I can hardly hear you. Anything wrong?"

Oh, how I wanted to tell him. Hear him say, "Everything will be okay, havaree. I'll be down on the next plane."

So why didn't I? I don't know. I just had this feeling that for once in my life I should try to go it alone. I was sick of being Goody Two Shoes.

"I told you I was sorry," I said. "How's Farfel?"

"*He* at least won't drive me to an early grave. This morning I taught him the word 'rakeek.' You know how he loves a biscuit. The minute I say it he sits up and begs."

"That's great, Dad."

"Yeah. Too bad I have to leave him in the kennel. He hates it."

The kennel. I caught my breath. I'd nearly forgotten that Dad was going up north. "When are you leaving?"

"Not sure yet. Car's all packed. If a couple of kids don't show up for bar mitzvah lessons, I'll get on the road before dinner. I didn't make a reservation, so I hope there's room at the lodge. If not I'll stay somewhere else and let you know. You have a good vacation, okay?"

He'd be gone. And I wouldn't even know where to find him. Maybe this was all a big mistake.

"Dad?"

"Yes, sweetheart?"

"Can you—can you answer a question?"

"I can try. What's it about?"

"A bird. An ideogram like in Egyptian hiero-glyphics or those symbols in ancient Chinese."

"That's your mother's department, not mine."

"But it's Hebrew. What does a red bird mean in Hebrew?"

The silence at the other end was eerie. I could almost hear my father breathe. "Red bird? Where did you see this red bird, Vivi?"

"This one's on a card."

"What card?"

"A Hanukkah card. It was on the floor. I mean, well, it really was on the sofa, but—"

"Never mind. Call Gram to the phone. I must speak to her right away."

"You can't. I mean, she's not here. She went up to the roof for a while."

"Well, go up there and get her. No, wait!" I could almost see him looking at the big gold pocket watch that used to belong to Grandpa. "I've got to run. My Torah class started two minutes ago. I'd better get to those kids before the walls tumble down like Jericho. Tell Gram I'll call her from the road."

"Okay. But Dad what about the b—?"

"Got to go now, sweetheart. Talk to you later."
His kiss slurped in my ear.

I rummaged in a drawer and found a swimsuit.

Hot pink bottoms and a big black bow where my bust might be someday. Last summer's Italian sensation. Ugh! My mom had picked it up in one of those little shops on the Via del Tritone in Rome, and Rachael had thrown it into my bag. I tossed it aside, pulled on my swim-team tank suit, grabbed a towel, and headed for the stairs to the roof.

"You just missed your grandma," a woman called from the far side of the pool. "She took the elevator down a minute ago." I thanked her and dived into the water. Gram would never believe I went swimming if my suit weren't even wet.

The water was tepid and the chlorine burned my eyes. I swam one lap, then treaded water, watching the action under the darkening sky. Two old men in terry robes sat hunched over a chessboard. Four women sat knitting in an arbor of potted palm trees. Around and around the edge of the roof, in the shadow of the bordering bougainvillea, a white-uniformed nurse pushed a frail old woman in a wheelchair.

At a flash of lightning, the nurse wheeled her charge toward the elevator. The women picked up their knitting baskets and left. But the two old men kept their eyes glued to the chessboard and never once looked up at the sky.

"You there. Get out of the water! You looking to get electrocuted?" It was the woman who'd spoken before. She motioned me toward the ladder, and I swam across the pool. As I drew closer, I recognized her from Goldstein's. She was lying in a chaise with her crutches on the ground nearby. Her dyed red hair was curled close to her head. The bright orange slash of her mouth looked like a wound on her floured, wrinkled face. She could have made a senior-citizen chorus line except for the cast on her leg. That was stretched out in front of her like a big white salami.

"I'm Sadie," she said. "You remember me? You had a good meal at Goldstein's?"

"Fine," I answered, holding onto the edge of the pool and kicking. "And you?"

Sadie frowned. "How can I enjoy anything while I have to hobble around on these crutches? First me, then Erica Steinhardt!"

"You were mugged too?"

Sadie sighed and pointed to her cast. "You think I got this from water skiing? I'm glad you're here. Maybe you can keep an eye on your grandma and make her stop running around alone. I told her, 'Tessie, you just can't do that anymore. The neighborhood's not like it used to be.' And you know what she did?"

I heaved myself up onto the concrete. "What?"

"She laughed at me."

That was no surprise. When Gram wasn't painting she was worrying about everyone else. There wasn't much time left over to fret about herself. I couldn't help smiling.

"Go ahead. Smile," Sadie said. "I suppose you're

just like her. You don't believe it could happen to you." She raised her voice twenty decibels and called to a man a few feet away. "It's Tessie Hartman's granddaughter, Mr. Johnson. She won't believe me. Tell her how it is around here." The man lowered his newspaper and looked at me.

"It's terrible," he said in a very loud voice. He pointed to a page of his newspaper. "See. It even says so right here. The Harborfront Hall condo area is the worst in the city for assaults. A woman was nearly killed the other day."

Sadie sighed. "It's too bad you had to move here now, Mr. Johnson. You should have lived here in the old days when a person could walk out at midnight and not be afraid."

The man almost dropped his newspaper. "A midnight raid?"

"Not RAID, Mr. Johnson. I said AFRAID." Sadie leaned toward me. "They're all the same, these men. Too vain to wear their hearing aids. Have to yell or they don't hear a thing." She shrugged. "What can you do?"

"Yes, Sadie's right. Even you," Mr. Johnson said. "Even young girls like you can be mugged. You should go home now while there's shtill time."

Shtill? The man's English had been perfect up till then. Where had that German accent come from? I stared at his sunburned face, the fleshy nose, his straight thin lips, and his cold gray eyes. He must have caught my look because he ducked behind his newspaper. All that showed were a few gray hairs combed sideways across his bald head.

The scene seemed to have gone right by Sadie. She picked up the conversation exactly where she'd left off. "And if you think the police will help you, you can forget it. All they keep saying is, 'Give them your purse.' So I did, and look at what happened." She pointed to her cast.

"They hurt you for no reason?"

Sadie shook her head and sighed. "It was raining cats and dogs that morning. They tried to grab my umbrella. God forbid they should get wet while they were robbing me. If I hadn't tried to hold onto it, maybe I wouldn't have landed on the ground. But it was my husband's umbrella. He should rest in peace, the dear."

"The police are here?" asked Mr. Johnson.

Sadie shook her head. "I didn't say POLICE. I said PEACE," she shouted. "I can't understand why those kids always wait for the rain. It was pouring the day they got Erica Steinhardt, too. She slipped and hit her head and ended up in the hospital, poor thing. A lot of good it did her that they never got her purse or her umbrella."

"What's this thing with umbrellas?"

Sadie shrugged. "Who knows? But nothing's what they got that time. A patrol car just happened by. The hoodlums saw it and took off like a bunch of horses at the track. Remember how fast they ran, Mr. Johnson?" she yelled.

The man's reply filtered through the newspaper. "I can't say. I wasn't there at the time."

Sadie's forehead puckered. "No? That's funny. I could have sworn I saw you in the crowd. Standing right between that dark-haired woman with the big straw hat and the Hasid with the long black coat. But it could have been someone else. My memory's like a tea strainer these days." She looked at me. "That's what happens when you get old." Her mouth stretched into a wide yawn. She lowered the back of her chair. "See? The sun is out again. Now it's safe to go for a swim. All that thunder and not even two drops of rain."

Mr. Johnson peered around his paper. "The cops again?" he whispered.

7

Gram came to the door wearing an apron. I followed her back to the kitchen, chasing down the smell of tomatoes and oregano. She went to the stove and stirred something in a big pot. I could almost taste the spaghetti and meatballs.

"I'm fixing tofu cacciatore," Gram said. "You'll love it, Vivi. Who needs meat with all that cholesterol? Go and relax. Dinner will be ready soon."

I stifled an expletive and drifted to the living room, where Gram's paintings stared down at me. Were they really so valuable that someone would kill for them? And if it was the art someone was after, why snatch umbrellas? No, it just didn't compute.

I found myself in front of *The Meeting*, looking at the kids in the schoolyard. Why were they standing in a circle with their heads bowed like that? There were so many "whys" and still no "becauses."

It was then that I noticed the girl and boy in the upper left-hand corner. They were walking hand in hand. Under the girl's blue lace cap, her hair was a mass of dark curls that fell in front of her eyes. I pushed back my own curls. Nothing could keep them in place either. Her navy skirt covered her knees, and her white sailor blouse lay flat on her chest. The top of her head just reached the boy's shoulder.

It looked like a nice shoulder to lean on. His face wasn't so bad either. Neither was the jet black hair peeking from beneath his deep blue skullcap with its red design in the middle. Gram had used a crimson paint that really caught the eye. But it wasn't the paint that made me catch my breath. It was the pattern.

I grabbed the back of a chair to keep from falling and looked at the picture one more time. There in the circle of kids I found them again—the same girl, the same boy—heads bowed down with the rest. There were ten kids altogether, enough for a minyan —a prayer group. But it couldn't be a minyan. No way. Back in those days, only the boys could be counted for that, and there were only six of them. Six boys with skullcaps, four girls with blue lace caps. And each cap was decorated with a tiny red bird.

Gram was rubbing a wooden bowl with garlic when I burst into the kitchen.

"Who's that girl in the painting?" I asked her, breathless.

My grandmother dumped a colander of lettuce into the garlicky bowl.

"Which painting is that?"

"The old one with the kids."

She picked up a cruet. "This dressing has all kinds of herbs and no salt. You'll love it, Vivi." She sprinkled the dressing over the salad. "I guess I didn't do such a great job," she said. "You couldn't even tell it was me."

I went to her and gave her a hug. "Of course I could. I was just checking. Who was the cute guy?" Her eyes clouded over but she smiled. "Don't tell me it's Grandpa?" I said.

"Who else could it be?"

"Wow! You guys were a pair! I bet you miss him a lot, huh?"

"Yes, my darling. There are times when I miss him dreadfully." She touched my cheek. "Forty-five years of togetherness is a long time."

I turned away. "Mom and Dad never even made it to ten. Guess people used to love a lot stronger in the old days."

"Oh, I don't know that love has much to do with it." Gram sighed. "Things were different then."

"How?"

"In lots of ways. I remember when I won the

scholarship to art school. Your grandfather was so happy for me. But once we were married it wasn't the same."

"What do you mean?"

Gram shrugged. "He felt it was his job to take care of me and my job to see to the family. A career for me was out of the question. Art was something to play with in my spare time. Oh, it wasn't all his fault. I suppose I felt that way too. It's just the way people thought back then." She wiped her hands on her apron. "Things aren't like that today. A woman wants to stand on her own two feet even while she's standing beside a man. Anything that gets in the way of her independence gets in the way of the marriage. Love alone isn't enough."

"That's weird coming from you."

"Weird? Why?"

"It's like something Mom once said. She told me her being in Paris had nothing to do with loving or not loving Dad."

"Your mother's a talented woman, darling, with a brain as well as a heart. She just wasn't cut out to be a rabbi's wife, spending her whole life in a con-gregational fishbowl. Will you never forgive her for that?"

I turned away. "No one forced her into it."

"No. It was a choice. One of those very hard, almost impossible choices. Come, let's eat. Everything is getting cold."

"No, wait! I have one more question. Why were

you kids in the painting all wearing blue caps on your heads, with those little red birds on top?"

Gram picked up the salad bowl, carried it to the table, and set it on the crisp, checkered cloth. "That, my darling, is a very long story."

"I have time."

"Yes. So you can wait." She sat down and began to chant in Hebrew. I joined her in the prayer of thanks: "Blessed be your name, O Lord our God, King of the Universe, who brings us bread from the earth." Gram cut a thick slice of seeded rye and handed it to me.

"You won't have to wait too long, my darling. I promise."

8

The note was on the kitchen table:

*VIVI—ORANGE JUICE AND
MILK IN FRIDGE. CEREAL IN
CUPBOARD TOP RIGHT OF
RANGE. HAD TO GO TO THE
STORE. DON'T LEAVE UNTIL
I RETURN.*

The brass hands of the old oak wall clock were at ten-fifteen. I stared again at the note.

"Had to go to the store." What store? Where? I had to get dressed. Go and find her. But sometime between putting on my left sock and my right sock, I realized how impossible it was. To go tearing around without knowing where to look was plain dumb. I put on my jeans and a shirt anyway, and I recited the morning prayer, adding a big P.S. "If you're not too busy this morning, God, could you please watch over Gram?"

I read the note again. I even filled a bowl with cereal but left it on the table. I went out onto the terrace, where I sat in the swing. That swing, hidden between the shimmering violet mimosa and the fiery bougainvillea, was once my secret place. I got up, paced around the garden, and, in the shadow of a trellis filled with hot pink clematis, I found the clumps of wild purple aster. "They gave me life," Gram had said.

I thought about how Gram had collected the seeds from an empty field in the Bronx. She brought them to Buffalo when she and Grandpa got married and went there to live. When my grandfather retired, they came down here and Grandpa brought the plants up the sixteen flights to the penthouse so Gram could have her garden in the sky.

I filled a watering can and was giving Gram's asters a drink when the *hoot hoot* of a boat drew me to the railing. On the ground below, white granite stairs led down to the bay, where small boats bobbed in the calm, inky water. The scene reminded me of another place, high above the Mediterranean Sea, where one can gaze down at the same kind of emerald-blue water. I sometimes stay there with my mother.

I wondered where my mother was now. Teaching her classes in Paris? At a language conference in Istanbul? She was right on time with her letters. There would probably be one waiting for me at home. Then I'd have to write back. It was always hard to think of something to say. What would it be this time? "Been to Florida—had a great time"? There was no way I would let her know how scared I was on the plane, how scared I am every summer flying halfway around the world to see her. The first time I was only seven. I clung to my father, screaming, "Please, Daddy, don't make me go!" And for a minute he'd held me close. Then, very gently, he unwound me and handed me over to the flight attendant.

"We promised," he said. "And a promise is a promise."

Why worry about it, I thought. I'd do what I always did—tell her only what I wanted her to know. I'm an expert at that. She would be glad I'd been to visit Gram. My mother likes Gram. Gram had never wrung her out like Grandpa had. I still remember him waving his arms and yelling: "Amicable divorce? A wife gets up one morning and says, 'Goodbye, got an offer to teach across the ocean.' Just like that she says it! And you're telling me the divorce was amicable? What about the child? Was the custody suit amicable too?"

Grandpa would never believe that the bargain they made really was simple—that Dad had offered

Mom a deal she couldn't refuse. She could have her freedom if he could have me. "It must have torn her to pieces," Gram had said just yesterday. But I knew my mother hadn't even put up a fight, and I'd never forgiven her for that. It was easy for Gram to talk, I thought, but she's not me. How could she know how I feel?

A warm breeze blew up from the ocean. A fishing boat chugged toward a pier. I saw the nets spread out to dry on the deck, and the people, like tiny dots. I remembered Mike's uncle and the strange mystery box in the newspaper clipping. Could the boat down there be *Noah's Ark?* I picked out a dot and pretended it was Mike. He was leaning against the rail, squinting at the sea. A dot with golden flecks in his eyes. The doorbell blasted me back to reality.

The cop at the door had a red face. He was big. One hand was at his neck, pulling on his collar as if it were too tight. In the other hand he held a small notepad.

"You Vivian Hartman?"

I stared at him.

"Miss," he said, "the lady two flights down—" He looked at the pad. "Sadie Marks. Said the victim lived alone but had a granddaughter visiting. Vivi. Short for Vivian, isn't it? That you?"

Victim? Gram? No, I thought, he couldn't have said that.

"She's still alive. They took her to St. Francis.

You are Vivian Hartman, aren't you?"

"Aviva."

"Thank you, Miss. I'm sorry. If you'll come with me. We have a car downstairs."

I still can't recall that ride. I can't recall much of anything before the green. Green walls, green doors. A green-gowned person lay in bed with tubes feeding into her arm. Bandages covered most of her face. It couldn't be Gram. Yet I knew it was.

I leaned over her. I took her limp hand. "Oh Gram, oh Gram," I whispered over and over. I must have sounded like a stuck record to the orderly who brought the baskets. "Thank you," I said, and I put the baskets on a table. One was full of fruit and had a bright yellow bow with a card attached.

"Wishing you a speedy recovery. The Harbor-front Hall gang." Sadie's name was there, and Arthur Johnson's, with a lot more names that I didn't know.

The other basket had green paper around it. There wasn't any card inside. I tore open the wrappings. Purple asters! I pushed aside some of the stalks. Still no card. Ouch! Something pricked my finger—a small sharp plastic rod. I tossed it into the wastebasket. There had to be a card somewhere, but I couldn't find one. My hands were shaking. My heart was a drum. Whoever had sent the basket was playing "Guess Who."

"O God," I prayed, "I guess you know what you're doing. But why for heaven's sake are you doing it to my gram? You have to know she's never harmed a soul in her life. Please, oh *please,* get her out of this mess alive. Just make her strong enough to eat again and I'll bring her kosher deli from Goldstein's every day." That made me feel I was helping a little bit anyway. But then I remembered something. "P.S.," I added, "I know that Goldstein's is pretty far away and I'm not allowed to drive, but don't worry. I'm the second fastest runner on the team."

It was all in his hands now. And God had to be better at his job than the police were at theirs. According to the report, a patrol car had got there fast but not before the kids had knocked Gram to the pavement. They'd sure done a job on her. And for what? An ugly old umbrella?

Poor Gram. Even the doctor couldn't do anything more. "Some people come out of a coma a lot sooner than others," was all he said. But I was a rabbi's daughter. I knew the truth. My father had sat at too many deathbeds where the person never woke up at all.

My father! Oh my God, I had to call him. This wasn't a kid thing anymore. It was a matter of life and death.

I picked up the phone and gave the operator Dad's number. No answer at the temple. He wasn't at home either. There was no way to reach him. He was somewhere on the road to Canada.

I felt Dad's hand on my shoulder. I heard his

voice—calm and reassuring. Then I put my head down, touched my lips to Gram's hand, and let the tears come full blast. I was bawling like a baby when I heard the knock on the door.

The next thing I knew, Mike was holding my hand. "Don't, Vivi, don't," he said. "Everything will be okay."

He was one big blur of white. I blinked him into focus. White shoes, white pants, white jacket. A ghost with a deep, gentle voice.

"They always need help at St. Francis," Mike said. "Whenever my uncle doesn't need me I volunteer. Just a gofer. I run things up from the lab and all that. I've been doing it for three years. I heard the name 'Hartman' in Emergency and panicked, thinking it was you."

I started to laugh, to giggle like I'd never stop.

"You're hysterical!" Mike was shaking me, rubbing my neck. Then he stood behind the chair and listened while my whole story gushed out. He never interrupted.

"Your grandmother will be okay," Mike said when I was done. "Try to hang in there. Get out of this room for a while. Walk around the halls. Anything. I have to get back to work now, but meet me later for dinner. The cafeteria's down in the basement. I'll be there around six." He hugged me. "Not to worry, eh?"

As Mike turned to go, he paused at the basket of flowers. "What do you know? Wild asters! I've never seen them growing down here. Wonder where they came from."

I sighed. "So do I. There wasn't a card."

"Maybe it fell off the tree. It happens all the time."

"Tree?"

"Those little plastic things. The florists stick them in the soil and attach the cards to them."

"You mean this?" I rummaged around in the wastebasket.

"Ouch!" A drop of blood squirted from my finger. I stared down at the plastic tree in my hand. A piece of red wire was fixed amid the tiny plastic branches.

Mike grabbed my hand. "Let me clean that scratch before it gets infected." He took a bandage from Gram's tray.

I pushed the bandage away and held up the wire. "Look at the shape!"

"The shape?"

"Of the wire! The red wire!" I thrust it under his nose.

Mike adjusted his glasses.

"Well I'll be darned. Looks like a little red bird."

"Yes." My voice shook. "Just like the one on your T-shirt." Mike's eyes widened. I sensed his panic. He masked it with a smile.

"That's Miami for you. Birds all over the place. See you later, eh?"

9

Gram and I were alone again. I looked from her face to the bland green wall. If only I could splash them both with color! My finger had stopped bleeding, but the spot pricked by the wire throbbed with a steady rhythm. Every pulse reminded me of the bird.

My eyes drifted to the basket of purple asters then wouldn't come unstuck. In a daze, I went to the basket and touched each blossom. I didn't even know I was counting them till I got to the last. There were just eighteen!

Eighteen! In Hebrew that number meant "life." Eighteen! It flew around my head, soaring and flapping on the wings of a mysterious red bird. Life!

Gram's painting, *Purple Asters*, had won her the scholarship to art school. It had opened up her life, she said. Whoever had sent the basket must have known that.

I tore away from the basket and collapsed in a chair. "Okay, Goody Two Shoes," I told myself, "time to try your hand at pilpul." Half an hour later I rang the bell for the nurse.

A chubby white form fluttered through the door to Gram's bedside. She took Gram's wrist.

"She's no worse, dear."

"Thank you, ma'am."

The nurse smiled. "Sister. Sister Jean."

"Sorry, I didn't know. I mean—well, you're my first nun."

"Can I get you anything?"

"No—I mean, yes. Her things. I'm looking for my grandmother's umbrella."

The nun shook her head. "Not here. The police took everything to examine for evidence. They always do. But don't worry, she won't need her things while she's here. I just told her gentleman friend the same thing."

"Gentleman? What gentleman?"

"He didn't leave his name. A nice chap. The old dear wanted to help by taking her things home. Your grandmother's very fortunate to have a friend like that."

"Fortunate?" I looked at Gram's pale, still body. What men did she know? Evan, the waiter at the deli? Mr. Johnson, the old guy from her building? I shivered. What if it was a man she didn't know? What if it was the Hasid? I turned to the nun.

"The man who spoke to you, Sister. Was he wearing a coat and hat?"

"A coat?"

"Yes. A long black coat. And a fur-trimmed hat."

"Here in Florida?" The nun touched my cheek. "You've been through a lot, dear. Try to get some rest and eat dinner. There's a good cafeteria in the basement. I'm going off duty now, but give me a ring when you're ready to go. A nurse will come to sit with your grandmother." She tiptoed out, her ample bosom leading the way.

I had to think. Ten minutes later, I was pressing the buzzer again. "Sister," I said to myself, practicing how to address her. But the person who came to the door didn't look like anyone's sister.

The sandy-haired, red-faced, white-coated giant swung past me, heading straight for Gram. "I say, has she awakened yet?"

I wondered if I was going crazy. Had the British invaded again? Torn down the flag? Made pudding of the Revolution? What were they all doing here?

"No," I told him. "She hasn't opened her eyes even once."

He held Gram's limp wrist. "Pulse is good." He checked the intravenous tubing, grunted, and tightened a valve.

"Name's Rockford," the nurse said, holding out

a massive hand. "Everyone calls me Rocky. Have you been here all day?"

I nodded. "Since early this morning."

"Anyone else come by?"

"Mike. I mean—a friend of mine. He works here. And when he heard the name Hartman, he—"

"Besides him."

"Only Sister Jean. And some man. I didn't see him. The sister said he wanted to help take Gram's things home."

"Oh?" The nurse smiled. He looked at his watch. "Well, I'm here to stay for a while. Ready for dinner, are you?"

I looked at Gram, hesitating.

He smiled. "Go now. I'll watch after her."

"Thanks. I really appreciate it." He nodded as I took a last look at my grandmother and stepped out into the hall. The wall clock said five thirty-five. My date with Mike was for six. First things first. There'd be just enough time.

A loudspeaker announced the end of visiting hours. Visitors moved toward the exits. Hoping no one would throw me out, I raced past the elevator, flew up the stairs, and burst onto the third-floor.

CRASH! A blond-haired candy striper was sprawled on the floor, her goodies dumped out beside her.

"Hey, I'm real sorry," I said. She rubbed her neck and got to her feet with a moan. I started to help her pick up her junk.

76

"It's about time you got here!" she said. "I sure can use the help, but I wish you new volunteers weren't so eager. Didn't they tell you anything in the office?"

I stared at her.

The girl sighed. "You get the candy and magazines downstairs in the gift shop. The female employees' lounge is the second door over there. The uniforms are on the rack. One size fits all. Now move it! Our shift started five minutes ago."

I watched her duck into a room. What a break! No nurse would try to hustle me out now. Even without the candy and magazines, I'd be safe in a candy striper's uniform.

The dresses were exactly where the girl said they would be. I put one on and checked it out in the full-length mirror. My disguise was perfect. Who would ever suspect a walking candy cane?

Out in the hall, aides scooted around with dinner carts. Nurses were shooing the last, straggling visitors out of the rooms. I put my head down and walked fast, trying to look like a person with a job.

As I passed the elevator, the light above it flashed red. Someone got out and fell into step behind me. I didn't dare breathe or turn my head, but I forced my shaky feet to go faster. The footsteps quickened and soon matched their rhythm to mine, clinging to my heels like a dark, eerie shadow.

10

I told myself it was dumb to be scared. What could happen to a person right in the middle of a hospital? But my legs kept trembling as I pushed them harder and harder. Erica's room, at last! I shoved aside a cart of empty dinner trays and dived through the half-opened door. SLAM!

A sharp pain tore through my forehead. I'd rammed into someone. I grabbed at her to keep myself from falling, and I got a fistful of long black hair. As the fuzzy image came clearer, I saw her face beneath the stiff nurse's cap. Good God, it was the woman from the airport!

For one eerie instant we stared at each other. Then footsteps sounded in the corridor. The woman shoved me aside and took off down the hallway. Through a misty haze, I watched her fly, a rocket on Bruno Magli heels.

The squeak of a rolling dinner cart made me jump. As I whirled around, a pale green blob came into focus. His black eyes glinted and his beard was moist with sweat. One corkscrew side curl had slipped out of his cap. So that's who'd been on my tail! The Hasid had cashed in his black coat and fur-trimmed hat for a surgeon's smock and stethoscope, but he wasn't looking to give me a checkup for gym. In fact, now that he had me he didn't seem to want me at all. With one good shove, he aimed the cart at my ribs, then tore down the hall after the woman. As he rounded the corner there was a loud, reverberating THUD! After that there was only silence, except for one sound—the *click, click, click* of Bruno Magli four-inch heels on a cold marble floor.

It wasn't until the footsteps faded that I heard the other sound—a low, agonizing moan from Erica's room. I stormed through the door. The pale old woman—her mouth gaping open—clutched the bedclothes, fighting for breath. Blood flowed from the bandage on her head. A pillow on the floor was bloody, too. "Tessie?" she said. The word was barely audible.

"No. It's me, Vivi." I grabbed the pillow, maneuvered it under her head, and reached for the call button.

"Stop! Don't ring!" The cry nearly did her in. She clutched my arm feebly, but it was too late. I'd already hit the buzzer. Erica fell back on the pillow. "They'll want to call the police. Don't let them! They'll ruin everything! You understand?"

I didn't. All I understood was that some crazy woman had tried to murder Erica and was probably on her way to finish off Gram. I'd never get there in time.

I grabbed the telephone. "Room 119. Please hurry."

"I didn't tell him anything," Erica whispered.

I covered the phone. "*Him*? You mean *her*, don't you? It was a woman."

"No, no, no!" Erica shook her head. "A man! With a stocking on his face." The phone clicked.

"Hello. Hello. Anyone there? It's Vivi Hartman."

"Rockford here."

"Thank God! How is she?"

"No change, love. These things take time. Nothing is likely to happen for days. Had your dinner?"

"Not yet. Listen. This is an emergency. Call hospital security. Tell them she needs protection. Then lock the door and don't let anyone in. I mean anyone at all! Understand?"

"I do."

"Thanks! And do me a favor, will you?"

"Sure, love. What?"

"Put a chair under the knob just to be sure! Like they do on TV."

"Anything you say. That all?"

"Yes. Thanks again." I hung up the phone.

"Evan?" Erica said. She started to cry. "I knew it. I just knew it. Something's happened to Tessie."

"I didn't say 'Evan,' I said 'again.' But you're right. Gram got mugged. She's down on the first floor. But she'll be okay," I said, with a lot more confidence than I felt.

"Tessie too! Oh my God! What will we do now? Where's the umbrella?"

"The police have it."

"The police? No police! No police. Please!"

"It can't be helped. The hospital has to report this attack."

"No, no. The police must know nothing. I'll tell the nurse I fell out of bed."

"Tell the nurse what you like, but tell me the truth. Why would someone try to kill you?"

Erica shook her head. "He's scared. Wants to stop us. But doesn't know who we are." She gasped for breath. "Wants me to give him the list." She reached into her gown and drew out a chain with a tiny brass key on the end.

"It's all in my trunk. Help us. Please help us. We're so very close."

"Close to what?" I wanted to know. I wanted to know everything. But the poor old woman seemed drained. "Just tell me one thing," I asked her. "Who would have sent Gram purple asters?"

Erica's eyes widened. "They already know about

Tessie?"

"They?"

"The group."

"Who are they?"

"Us. Picture," she managed to say. "Back. Don't let him find the list." Her head fell back against the bloody pillow. "Nurse coming. Go. No police! Promise!"

"I promise," I whispered. But only for now, I told myself, as I started down the corridor. I remembered the time the swastika had been painted on our door with the words "DIRTY JEWS" splashed in red. The cops had helped clean up the mess and had caught the kids who'd done it. And the time that Farfel got lost and a policeman found him hanging out in an old abandoned doghouse. I even remembered the officer who came to my kindergarten eight years ago and told us kids that the police were our friends. How had they suddenly become the enemy?

I used the phone in the lounge to call Gram's room. Rocky's voice was comforting. "All's quiet. Did you eat your dinner yet, love?"

"No, not yet. Any disturbance at all?"

"Not a soul came by."

"Not even security?"

"Security? Oh, sure. Enjoy your dinner, love. Security's the best."

I doused my face with cold water. Even the sandpapery towels felt good. It was five past six. Mike would be waiting. A shudder passed through me as I remembered his T-shirt with the red bird and his panic when I asked about it. But if I didn't go, how would I ever find out anything?

He was standing in the cafeteria's doorway, rocking back and forth on his toes. In spite of everything, it felt good to see him again.

"You going in for candy stripes, eh?"

"You don't like it?"

"No. I mean, yes. I do. It's nice. You decide to join us volunteers?" I explained about the uniform as we went to the counter. It was a long walk along the display case to find some food not completely forbidden.

"How about the peanut butter and jelly?" Mike asked. It wasn't spaghetti and meatballs but it would do. He tossed me an apple, plopped a carton of milk on my tray, flashed his I.D., and led the way to a table. What should I say? How much should I tell him? What did he already know? I might as well go for broke, I decided. Tell him everything, and watch for his reactions.

All through dinner he listened as I brought him up to date on my adventures. He never blinked an eye when I came to the woman with the hat. But my visit to Erica finally got a rise.

"What made you go to see her?" he asked.

I picked up my sandwich. "To find out about the umbrella, of course."

"Umbrella? What umbrella?" His innocent look

83

could have fooled 007.

"The one the police have now. I figured it had to be part of the whole thing. Look at it this way. One, Sadie gets mugged. The kids go for her purse but they also try to steal her umbrella. Two, there's Erica. She gets mugged in the rain. She's also carrying an umbrella. But the police come too fast. The thieves don't get anything. Which leaves us with three—Gram. She's out on a sunny morning. And of all the people around, they pick her to mug. Why?"

Mike shrugged. "She had a big fat purse?"

"No. A big ugly umbrella. She carries it around for shade."

Mike shook his head. "I don't know. The whole thing sounds crazy to me."

If all this was a put-on, he was a darn good actor. He could have won an Emmy.

"Maybe," I said, "but there's something else, too. Call it number four. When Gram and I were visiting Erica, she seemed pretty beat up but not too beat up to worry about the umbrella. She told Gram not to hang it on the back of the chair because she might forget it."

"And that's why you went through all that garbage to see Erica?"

"No. There was another reason, too. The purple asters."

"Okay, Sherlock Holmes. How do they fit in?"

"That's easy. One, whoever sent the asters had to

have known about Gram's scholarship to art school. Two, they must have known her well. Well enough to know that she felt it had opened up her life."

"You figured that out from the asters?"

"Yes. Don't you see? There were exactly eighteen of them."

"Eighteen! That's *hai*. It means life. You're a genius, Vivi." I couldn't believe it. He sounded so sincere he caught me off guard.

"No. Just a pilpul pro."

Mike stared. "That old Torah logic? Where in the world did you ever learn that?"

I felt my face burning. "Never mind. Anyway, I never learned much from Erica, and I wound up making that stupid promise about the police." Mike's face seemed to relax.

"But I just may not keep it," I said.

He put down his sandwich. "You're going to go back on your word?"

"Not right now." I touched the tiny key hanging on the chain around my neck. "Not until I see what's in that trunk. After that—"

"You can't call them, Vivi. Even after that." Mike held my eyes with his. "A promise is a promise." He sounded like my father.

"I wonder if Rocky would stay with Gram while I go back to the apartment," I said. "I feel she's safe with him there."

"Rocky?"

"The nurse who's sitting with Gram. You know something? He's the first male nurse I've ever met."

"Oh, no!" Mike was out of his seat, running toward the exit. "There are no male nurses at St. Francis!"

I flew up the steps past a man in a gray uniform and exploded into Gram's room. Past the person in the chair, the table with the phone, the basket of fruit, and the eighteen purple asters.

"Oh, Gram, thank God you're alive!"

"And why shouldn't she be, dear?" asked Sister Jean. The nun had left her chair and was standing at my side. Mike was checking Gram's intravenous tubing. Rocky wasn't anywhere around.

"I came back for my book and found the buzzer ringing," the sister said. "But when I got to your grandmother's room she was all alone except for Fred, the guard on duty outside. Fred told me that someone had rung up his portable phone. Told him to stay outside her door through the night. The chap gave the name 'Rockford' and had a very British accent."

"British?" Mike asked. "What did the guy look like?"

"Fred never saw him. He couldn't tell me that."

"I can," I said. "Rockford was tall, big shouldered, and fair. He had blue eyes and a square chin. He looked just like the tourist who bumped into you at the airport. And just like Evan, the waiter at Goldstein's. It's as if they were clones, all cut from

86

the same mold." I looked for Mike's reaction.

"Really?" was all he said. Mike turned to Sister Jean. "Vivi wants to go back to Harborfront Hall for a while," he told her. "I'm going to give her a lift on the bike."

"Oh, no!" I shouted. "That's really not necessary. It's just a short taxi ride."

"Don't be silly, child," said the nun. "You never know who you're getting for a driver. Micah can get you there nice and safe. I'll stay here with Mrs. Hartman and read." She pointed to her book. "Nothing like a good mystery, and I've got a bit to go till the end."

11

"Good evening, señorita," Pedro said, touching his cap. He was speaking to me but he didn't take his eyes off Mike. "Señora Hartman—she'll be all right?"

I tried to smile. "I hope so, Pedro. Do you think you could let me in? I forgot the keys Gram gave me." The elevator operator eyed Mike again and frowned.

"You go home, señor?"

"Pretty soon," Mike said. The elevator stopped. Pedro unclipped a key from a bunch on his belt.

"The master," he said, and opened both locks in a flash.

"Thanks," I told him.

Pedro looked at Mike. "In a little while you ring and I take you down. Si?"

Mike shrugged. "Si."

Pedro walked back to his elevator, shaking his head.

"Maybe si. Maybe no," Mike sang out from the foyer. He collapsed on a bench and doubled over in laughter. "The old guy thinks I'm out to ravage you." I didn't answer. It wasn't all that funny to me. Having Pedro worry about me made me feel a little safer.

The apartment felt empty without Gram. I got a couple of Cokes from the fridge and led the way to the blue room.

"You sure you want to do this?" Mike asked.

I pulled the gold chain over my head. "Sure." I clutched the key hard to keep my hands from shaking, and I plunged it into the tiny rusty lock. I turned the key and pushed at the lid of the trunk. Nothing happened.

"Wait. There are side clasps," Mike said. He pulled the brass rings, and the old trunk groaned as the lid escaped from its bindings. I lifted the heavy cover slowly. Ugh! It smelled like mothballs.

I pulled out some woolen sweaters. A layer of books came next. Tolstoy, Goethe in German, a Hebrew biography of Herzl, a dog-eared English copy of *Tom Sawyer.* Beneath that, more clothing— a woman's army uniform. A greenish skirt, shirt, jacket, and beret.

Mike picked up the hat and looked at the patch.

"Holy Moses! She must have been in the first Israeli Defense Force, the old Haganah."

I dug deeper and came up with a bunch of letters wrapped in a man's white handkerchief. As I started to unwrap them, I spotted a crusty notebook sealed in a plain plastic storage bag. The Hebrew writing showed right through it: ERICA STEINHARDT, MY DIARY. I dropped the letters and went for the book, opening the bag gingerly.

The book smelled like my father's old gardening shoes. The pages crackled when I turned them, and the few I leafed through were blank. Then I realized that a Hebrew book would begin at the other end. I turned to the back where the writing began and noticed another weird thing about this diary. Most diaries start on New Year's Day with a bunch of resolutions no one keeps. Erica's diary began in November.

"Are you going to keep it all to yourself?" asked Mike, sitting cross-legged on the rug, "or are you going to clue me in?" I settled down beside him and started to read aloud.

ERICA STEINHARDT AGE TEN YEARS
MY OWN JOURNAL
1 NOVEMBER 1938
I am starting this journal because Mama said I must practice writing so I will not forget how while I do not go to school. No Jewish children can go to

school anymore, only real Germans. Our new leader, Mr. Hitler, said Jews aren't real Germans. My Papa told me Mr. Hitler is angry because our country lost the big war that happened before I was born. Many real Germans and many Jewish Germans are poor since the war. But Mr. Hitler said the Jews are all rich and they are to blame for all the trouble so no Jewish children are allowed to go to school.

I am writing in Hebrew because real Germans cannot read Hebrew. If the police find my book they will not know what I say. Then maybe they will not arrest me like they did the Hebrew School teacher. Yesterday the policemen came into our class and threw him down on the floor. They dug their heels into his face and pulled his beard. Then they took him away. I was so scared I hardly breathed. My Papa said it was because my teacher spoke out and told what he thought. I think if he had said it in Hebrew instead of German the policemen would not have understood so they would not have arrested him. Now there is no more Hebrew School either.

I looked at Mike. "My God. No wonder she has this thing about police!"

"Right. Do you see why you can't call them?" he answered. "The old girl would have hysterics."

"Maybe." I turned back to the diary.

10 NOVEMBER 1938

My Papa took me to the Fasanenstrasse where the synagogue is where we pray. But the stained glass windows are broken and most of the building is burned down. Some kids from my old class were running around but they didn't talk to me. They yelled, "Judenrein! Judenrein! We're rid of the Jews!" I tried not to cry. I used to think they liked me.

Somehow I got through the rest of the story—about them going to the father's store, or what was left of it. The sign—JACOB STEINHARDT, FINE CHINA, SILVER, AND CRYSTAL—was lying smashed on the ground. "The fine china, silver, and crystal belong to the real Germans now," Erica had written. It was the evening after Kristallnacht, the Night of Broken Glass. All the Jewish-owned stores were destroyed. "It's only the beginning," her father told her. "We will have to leave Germany."

Mike got up and stared out the window. As I read the next part he didn't look at me.

12 NOVEMBER 1938

I'm too big to cry but I cry just the same. I do not want to leave my house and my friends. Mama does not want to leave her garden. Papa is sad too. I can tell by the way he rubs his beard all the time. Only Marcus isn't sad. He's too little to know we must go to America. Papa said it's a country where the people are free and his sister in America will help us. There is a cousin my age called Benjy.

Benjy? Of course! She was talking about my grandfather! That made Erica my cousin too. I touched my lips to the diary, feeling a stronger connection.

25 NOVEMBER 1938
Papa can get only one visa for America. He said we are lucky to get even that. But who should be the one to go? Mama cannot leave Marcus because Marcus is a baby. I guess it will be Papa. Oh, my darling Papa, without you how will I live?

23 DECEMBER 1938
It's the first night of Hanukkah. We sang and played with the dreidels and Papa picked me to light the candles. He gave me ten whole deutsche marks. But how can I spend them? He picked me to go to America, too. I cried and cried but he would not listen. I was missing too much school, he said. In America I would be free. I would go to school and learn and he and Mama and Marcus would follow later.

I found a tissue and wiped my eyes. "It's your turn," I said. Mike came to me slowly and took the book. In a soft, fluent Hebrew he described a day, January tenth. There was a new cover of snow on the ground. Kids were laughing, pelting each other with snowballs on their way to school, but all Erica felt was the cold. She was going to the train. At the station, her parents kissed her goodbye. She hugged her little brother. A female friend of the family was going, too, and they'd share a room. The train would take them to Cherbourg, France, where the ship would be waiting.

I thought maybe we wouldn't find it and would have to go back home. But we found it. Then I thought they would see my passport with the "J" for Jew stamped on it, and they wouldn't let me on the ship so Papa would have to come and get me. But it's an English ship, not German. It's name is the Queen Mary. *It's very big. There are other children here but we cannot speak together. One is Russian, one is French, another is Polish. We play tag together sometimes.*

"You okay now?" Mike asked so gently that, for a time, all suspicion of him left me.

"I guess so." I took the book. The date of the entry was January twentieth. Erica had been in America four days.

My aunt and uncle and my cousin Benjy met me. They took me to the Bronx, a part of America in New York City. They are very good to me. Already they brought me a friend. Her name is Tessie. Tomorrow we will go to school together.

The ancient script blurred with my tears then came into focus again. School was no ballgame for Erica. Because she didn't know English, they threw her into first grade and treated her like she was retarded.

The other children laugh at me because I am so big and don't know how to say anything.

Mike went to the kitchen and brought me back a glass of water. "Sure you want to go on?" I wasn't sure but I knew I couldn't do anything else. So I picked up the notebook again.

Tessie has many friends. The leader is my cousin Benjy. Now they are my friends, too. When the other children laugh at me the boys in our group fight them. Then they do not laugh anymore. Only one doesn't fight. He teaches me English. His name is Patrick O'Riley. His sister is called Jean. They are both very nice.

Patrick? The one my father was named for? I clutched the old notebook harder. "We've almost got it!"

Mike looked over my shoulder. "Got what?"

"Their names. She's talking about 'the group,' didn't you hear? Oh, Mike, I hope you're not falling asleep. Here, why don't you read again?" I held out the book.

18 APRIL 1939

What a beautiful spring. What a wonderful Passover. Tessie won a scholarship to art school and I got a letter from Mama. They have their visas at last. But not for the United States. No Jews can get these. The United States says it doesn't have room for them yet. So Mama and Papa and Marcus will go to Cuba and wait. Cuba is only ninety miles from Florida and Florida is part of the United States. They will sail there on a German ship. It's name is—

Mike's face went white. He almost dropped the diary. I took it from him and found the place he'd left off.

It's name is the St. Louis.

I couldn't say it aloud. The blue room disappeared. I was back home in Hebrew School. The course was Holocaust I, my father's class. A black-and-white movie was on the screen. I saw a big ship flying a Nazi swastika. The decks were packed with people.

"Who are those people, Rabbi Hartman?" someone asked.

My dad's voice was hoarse. "Jewish refugees. They were trying to land in Cuba."

"How come they're anchored so far out in the harbor?"

"The Cubans didn't let them come closer than that."

The scene changed. I saw the deck clearly and looked at the faces of the refugees. Some were crying, others tried to smile. Still others stared off into space. Some small boats came into view, swarming around the ship. Fishing dinghies were jam-packed with people waving to those on the ship.

"They're the relatives and friends of the passengers on the *St. Louis*," my father said. "They came every day and shouted encouragement." Barry Silverstein, the class nerd, raised his hand. He was always asking questions right at the end of the period and made us all late for our next class.

"How long were they stuck there before they finally got in, Rabbi Hartman?"

"A year and a half, like we'll be stuck here if you keep asking questions!" someone whispered. But for once my dad hadn't gone on and on. His face became pale, his eyes narrowed.

"Literacy's a wonderful skill, Silverstein," he said. "You were supposed to have read chapter thirty-four in the text. Make sure to have it done by tomorrow. That goes for all of you. Maybe then we can discuss it."

The chime of the grandfather clock in the hall brought me back to the present. Mike was at the window looking out to the bay. I started to read aloud again, but it didn't sound like me.

19 APRIL 1939

Oh, how I want to go to Cuba and meet my family when they land. But how can I go without any money? Today Benjy saw me crying and told me not to be sad. He said the group will get me the money to go. Myron Goldstein, one of the friends, has an idea for a raffle. Everyone will buy tickets and a lucky one will win a prize. That's how people get money in America.

Goldstein? The deli guy! I thought.

10 MAY 1939

We have much money. Enough for me to go to Cuba. I was so happy but now I am sad again. My uncle will not let me go alone. He says he must come too, but there is not enough money for both. We cannot sell more raffles because Mary Jane Watkins already won the prize. It was a ticket to the movies.

12 MAY 1939

Today Patrick saw me crying. He dried my eyes with his handkerchief. Then he told me not to worry. In his church is a box where people put money to help others. Patrick will ask the priest for the money in the box so my uncle can come with me to Cuba.

14 MAY 1939

Patrick had to stand in front of everyone in the

98

church. He had to make a speech. His sister Jean told me he was scared. After the speech, she said, people put money in the box. When the priest looked in the box he said Patrick should grow up to be a priest. He said Patrick could even be a bishop.

Was that why Patrick became a priest? I wondered. I wondered how he got to be a bishop. And I wondered why no one ever told me why they'd given my dad his name. I was deathly afraid to read the rest of the diary. But I couldn't stop, either.

23 MAY 1939

I cannot sleep. Tomorrow I must wake up very early but I will already be awake. My uncle and I will go on the train to Florida. Then we will sail on a boat to Cuba. My uncle said it will be a little boat, not big like the Queen Mary *or* St. Louis. *But the trip is not long. We will be there in three days, in plenty of time to meet Mama, Papa, and Marcus. Patrick gave me a book,* Tom Sawyer, *to read on the way.*

I turned to the next page. It was blank. I turned another, and the one after that. I tore through the book to the very last one. It was just as naked as the rest.

Mike came over and took the diary, put it back in its plastic bag and into the trunk. I picked up the sweaters and other books and put them in too. All except *Tom Sawyer.* I opened it and read the inscription. "To Erica. Have a wonderful trip. Love, Pat." I put it on top of everything else and was about to lock the trunk. Then I noticed the package of letters in the handkerchief. I laid them alongside *Tom Sawyer* and locked the trunk with the key.

I thought about the group. A few had been mentioned in the diary. Who were the rest? I pictured the young Erica, then I thought of the Erica I knew—old and sick. I heard her voice whispering, "Picture." But I'd looked at the picture so many times. What more could it tell me? Then I heard the other word, "Back." Back? Of course! That was it!

"You ready to go?" Mike asked me.

"Almost," I answered. "There's just one more thing I have to do. Come here. Help me with this."

Together we took down the painting, leaned it on the couch, and turned it over. Pasted to the back was an old yellowed envelope. I carefully removed the sheet of paper from inside.

They were all there—all the names I knew and some I'd never heard of. I started saying each one, savoring the sounds, working my way down the list.

"Holy Moses, haven't you had enough?" Mike said. "Let's get out of here." There was a catch in his voice. I stopped reading, folded the list, and slipped it into its envelope—but not before I'd spotted the name "Abramson."

"C'mon," I whispered, lifting the painting to the

wall. "Let's get the old team back where they belong."

12

I took off my shoes. I needed to run. The damp, gritty sand crunched under my feet. Mike caught up, grabbed my hand, and together we flew to the water. We stood there breathing the moisture, listening to the crashing waves. We watched the moon play hide-and-seek with the clouds while the ocean licked our feet. Then we walked and walked and walked.

"They never got off that ship in Havana," I said. "She never got to touch them. Never got her family back again."

"I know," Mike whispered.

I froze. Had he known about Erica all along?

"I know all about the *St. Louis*," he said.

"From that history book you had on the plane?" I asked him, praying that the knowledge was purely academic.

"No."

"Is that all you can say?"

He shrugged. "I'm tired. Aren't you?" He took off his sweatshirt and spread it out on the damp sand. He dropped down and pulled me down beside him. "Ever been to Havana?"

I shuddered. "Of course not. It's Communist and full of drugs. Who'd want to go there?"

"My uncle."

I looked at him. "For goodness' sake, why?"

"I don't know. Only I think it has something to do with the *St. Louis.* I heard him say something about finding more witnesses. It was anchored off Havana for seven days. Remember?"

"Sure. The Cubans were partners with the Nazis. They wouldn't let the refugees in. No one got off the ship except a few officers who the police took back and forth from ship to shore."

"Yeah, that's right." Mike caught my hand. "Only those so-called officers were actually Nazi spies."

"Spies?"

"You better believe it. That's why Hitler let the ship leave in the first place. His 'officers' spread anti-Semitic propaganda into Cuba and the U.S. Then they brought U.S. military secrets back out. It was all laid out on microfilm they hid inside canes and umbrellas."

"Umbrellas?" I caught my breath.

Mike sighed. "After seven days the dirty work was finished and Hitler ordered the *St. Louis* back to Germany. Well, you know the rest."

I pulled my hand away and hugged myself trying to get warm, but shivers ran up and down my spine. I was back in Buffalo doing my homework for Hebrew School. I was reading about the ship and its captain, Gustave Schroeder—one sweet guy, not a Nazi. Nine hundred and seven men, women, and little kids going back to be killed in concentration camps didn't sit well with the captain's conscience. So he turned the ship around and headed for Miami, only ninety miles from Cuba. With his ship anchored in the bay and the coast guard all around, the captain sent frantic wires to Washington. But Hitler's propaganda had gotten there first: The Jews would steal jobs. The Jews would take over the country. The Jews would get America into a war.

Mike put his arm around me. "You cold?"

"A little. I always am when I think about that story."

Mike kicked the sand. "Hitler couldn't have planned it any better if he'd tried, eh? And boy, did he let the whole world know about it. I can just see the headlines: U.S. REJECTS THE *ST. LOUIS*. REFUGEES SENT BACK TO DIE, SHUNNED BY THE WORLD'S GREATEST DEMOCRACY.

What a laugh the Führer must have had."

I looked out at the ocean. I could almost see the ship anchored there, with its tired, hopeless passengers. They cried, prayed, threatened suicide. The United States of America was their only hope. Surely the country wouldn't lock its gates. But it had.

I didn't believe all the hatred had come from the outside. Americans had minds of their own, didn't they? Since the day of that assignment for Holocaust I, I'd never forgiven my country for the *St. Louis*.

A faint breeze blew. A large gull swooped to the water, falling on some unsuspecting prey. "Tell me about the spies and the umbrellas," I asked Mike.

He looked at his watch. "Some other time." He stood up. "Let's go get something to eat. I'm starving. Ever been to the Scalawag Shack? It's the best darn deli on the beach—my uncle's favorite hangout."

I shook my head. "I'll take a rain check. I've got to get back to the hospital. But first I have to change these sneakers. They're dripping with wet sand."

The moon went into hiding somewhere behind a cloud as we headed toward Harborfront Hall. Everything was black and quiet. Except for the squishing of my sneakers, I didn't hear a sound. The courtyard was so empty you could drive a bulldozer through it without hitting a soul. Even the breeze had died, like it sometimes does just before a storm. I was glad to reach the lobby, to stand beneath the bright lamp and press the button for the elevator.

"It's not working, miss," the doorman said. "Too late to see about it tonight. You can take the self-service as far as fifteen, but you'll have to use the outside steps from there." I groaned and signed out a master key.

"Stop complaining," Mike said. "Compared to dealing with that Pedro fellow, the outside staircase will be a breeze. Where does it end up, on the terrace?"

I nodded, saving my breath for the stairs.

In the dark, the terrace looked creepy, but the wonderful smells soothed me. I took Mike's hand, led him through the maze of flowers, and used the master key on the door. "Hurry," Mike said, checking his watch. "I'm famished." He charged past me into the living room and plopped down on the rug.

I went to the den, opened the closet, and reached on the shelf for my other pair of sneakers. My heart did a cartwheel.

The sneaker was empty. The orange dress from Hong Kong was hanging on the crossbar with my shirts. And the shirts weren't in their right order, either. A yellow shirt was next to a red one, with a white shirt on the other side. I flew to the bureau. My drawers were a mess, too—scarves where socks should have been. Someone had done a number on my room then tried to straighten it again. But the crazy thing was nothing seemed to be missing.

I checked out the desk. The card with the red bird was still there. Then I made a dash for the blue room and opened the trunk. The diary was there in its plastic bag, but *Tom Sawyer* was under the uniform. The letters were still wrapped in the handkerchief.

"You ready yet?" Mike called. I went to the living room. He was lying on the rug watching TV. "What's wrong? You're pale." He followed me to the kitchen. Nothing disturbed there. Gram's room seemed okay too.

"For God's sake, Vivi, what happened?"

I took a breath. "Someone's been here."

"You sure?"

"Absolutely. Things aren't the way they were. But the strange thing is nothing seems to be gone."

"Your grandma have a maid?"

"A once-a-week type," I said.

"Could she have been in dusting?"

I didn't know much about maids, but that didn't make sense at all. "I doubt it," I said, straightening one of the pictures on the wall. "What maid would come at night?" I stood back and looked at the picture. It was *The Meeting,* and it was still a little crooked. *The Meeting*! Oh my God! I took down the painting, turned it over, and felt inside the old yellowed envelope. It was empty.

Someone had stolen the list. The same man

who'd attacked Erica? Was he going to go after all of them now?

But how could he have gotten in? I went to the foyer and opened the door. The locks seemed okay. I picked up the night-edition *Herald* Pedro had thrown on the bench. Instinctively, I turned toward the elevator. The doors were slightly ajar. Sticking out between them was a gray pant leg that ended in a black patent leather shoe. Only one person I knew had shoes so shiny you could almost see your face in them. At the toe of Pedro's shoe lay his belt—but its ring of keys was gone.

"Push the button!" Mike yelled from behind me. He ran out and grabbed hold of the shoe.

I pushed and the door slid open. Pedro's back was propped against the right wall of the elevator. His head drooped down with his hat still on it. I glued my finger to the STOP button while Mike dragged Pedro out into the hall. Mike was on his knees in a second, slapping the old man's face.

"Wake up!" Mike said. "Wake up!" Pedro made a sound, a cross between a whinny and a moan. His nose twitched and he was quiet again. Mike leaned back and gulped in air. Then the phone rang. With shaking fingers, I picked up the extension on the credenza.

"It's Martin, the doorman. Just wanted to tell you the elevator's working again."

I thanked him, clicked off, and dialed "O" for an operator.

"What are you doing?" Mike whispered.

"Calling the police."

"No!" He dropped Pedro and grabbed the phone from my hand. "You promised. A promise is a promise."

"Except when it's a matter of life and death," I answered.

Mike looked at Pedro. "He's not dead. He even spoke. You heard him. He's just conked out. Like he's sleeping."

Sleeping? Pedro was sleeping? He'd gone to bed in the elevator with his cap on his head and his foot hanging out the door?

Mike lifted Pedro's cap. "Come here. Have a look." I examined the front of the old man's head where a scab had begun to form. Below the scab, a swollen blue lump protruded through Pedro's splotchy skin. I was about to be very sick.

"How can you be so sure he's only sleeping?" I managed.

Mike shrugged. "He's breathing fine. Whoever did it just wanted in. The old guy must have got in the way." He touched the lump gently. "Could use something cold on it."

I hobbled to the freezer and came back with Gram's better-than-aspirin, new-fangled plastic ice pack.

"Coffee would help, too." I turned back toward the kitchen then stopped. "But not the kind we have. Gram only uses decaf."

Mike wiped his forehead. "Oh, great!"

"But maybe I can get the real stuff from Sadie," I told him.

"Who?"

"Sadie." I was already out the door. "The neighbor two flights down."

After five long rings, the door opened. I tried not to stare at Sadie's white flannel nightgown or the pink plastic curlers sticking out all over her orange head.

"At this time of night you're serving coffee?" she said. "Isn't it time your boyfriend went home?"

"But—"

"No 'buts.' You think I didn't hear you? I was out on my patio getting some air when you two came sneaking up the back stairs. That's the way to behave behind your poor grandmother's back?"

My heart stopped beating. "You heard us? Tell me, did you hear anything else? Anyone before that?"

Sadie sniffed. "You had a few before him? One boyfriend isn't enough?"

I stamped my foot. "Mike's not my boyfriend. And we're leaving soon anyway. We're going back to the hospital. He works there."

"He's a doctor? Why didn't you say so?" Sadie started for the cupboard.

"No, a student."

She got out a package of coffee and put it into my hands. "Don't worry. Soon he'll be a resident."

As she opened the fridge I turned and fled. But her voice reached me halfway down the hall. "Maybe he'd like a piece of my apple cake too?"

Pedro didn't fight the strong black coffee we fed to him with a spoon, though at first he nearly choked on it. We stood him up and dragged him around, stopping periodically to give him another sip. It was a good five minutes before he opened his eyes.

I searched his face. "What happened, Pedro?" He held out his hands, shook his head, and sighed.

Mike patted the old man's arm and winked at me. "Maybe you got dizzy—fell and hit your head, eh, Pedro?" I bit my lip to keep from shouting, "No!"

Pedro shrugged.

"Have some more coffee," Mike offered. "Just a little dizzy spell. Nothing to worry about. You live far from here, señor?"

Pedro didn't live far. He lived right downstairs in a small basement apartment behind the garage. Wrestling with a number-ten guilt trip, I helped Mike get him there. I felt guilty for letting Gram go out alone and get mugged, for letting poor Pedro believe a lie, and for letting Mike get away with it, just so the old man wouldn't call the police. Most of all, I felt guilty for not having called the police myself. Yet calling them would have made me feel guilty, too—guilty about the promise I'd made to Erica.

13

"Hey, stop worrying. The old guy will be as good as new by tomorrow," Mike said as we walked away from Harborfront Hall.

"But he could have been dead."

"Yeah, well—if I don't get a pastrami sandwich soon, I'll be dead of malnutrition. Why don't you come with me?"

"Thanks, but I've got to get back. I'll eat at the hospital."

"The St. Francis cafeteria? It's the pits this late at night. Come to the Scalawag Shack. We'll call and check on your grandma from there."

I was starved and exhausted. Mike had been odd, but so far not a threat. A short break seemed to make sense. A few minutes later I was flying through the dark, leaning into Mike's back. "You okay?" he asked.

The salt wind whipped my face, carried my "Slower, please!" away. I pressed my nose against his shirt and prayed.

God was kind. We got there. And across from the deli was a phone booth. Mike parked the bike while I dialed. Sister Jean's voice was warm at the other end.

"Her condition hasn't changed, dear. Don't you worry, now. I'll be here through the night. Have a happy holiday."

"Holiday?" I stared at the phone. "Oh, yes. Holiday. Thank you, Sister." I hung up, stepped outside, and looked at the line of people waiting to get inside the restaurant. In the window of the Scalawag Shack, a giant menorah poured its miracle light on some plastic corned beef sandwiches. The bumps of a plaster hallah shone with varnish. I was looking at a platter of clay bagels when Mike came out of the parking lot. He grabbed my hand and rushed me toward the line.

"Happy Holiday, Micah," I said.

He looked at me and then up at the sky. "Well, how about that, eh? There are at least three stars. Happy Hanukkah, Vivi." Then he kissed me. Me, Vivi E. Hartman. A shower of polyester snowflakes cascaded from the roof of the Scalawag Shack, sprinkling our hair with glitz. But Mike had kissed me. All the man-made muck in the universe couldn't stop me from feeling real.

I didn't even care that the whole line was watching us. I didn't know someone else was watching too. But Mike must have seen him because, all of a sudden, he dropped me like a pizza just out of the oven.

Bushy brown eyebrows couldn't hide the twinkle in the man's eyes. His thick chestnut hair reached to the edge of his collar, parting at one ear where a gold earring glistened. He laughed and held out a weathered hand. "You must be Vivi. I'm Micah's uncle, Noah."

So this was the man behind the mystery box. I hadn't even figured out his accent when he took each of us under an arm and moved like he was going to storm a wall. Most people just stared, but one lady started to yell.

"Hey, those kids were way back there. Who do they think they are rushing the line?"

"My children by my first wife," Noah shouted. "I get them every holiday. What can I do?" His accent was Israeli with a deeper Bronx tinge than Mike's.

The Scalawag Shack was no Goldstein's Deli. The employees didn't wear skullcaps and beards, but miniskirts and very sheer hose. A person could eat anything anywhere.

"Give me the special," Noah said, and he excused himself to make a call.

The waitress turned to me. "It's kosher-style pastrami on rye today, just like your mother makes." Obviously she didn't know my mother. She didn't know me either. Kosher-style might taste a lot like kosher, but the rules say it's not in the same league. In a place like this I couldn't even eat spaghetti and meatballs.

"A bagel and lox," I said. The waitress took Mike's order and left. But a few minutes later she was back, handing Noah an envelope.

"From the lady who just came in," she said, pointing toward a red leather booth. Noah looked at the woman, winked, and opened his letter. Mike glanced at her and nodded. I looked in her direction and my heart did a flip-flop. I couldn't see her face, but who could miss that hat and fabulous long black hair?

"Boss in the kitchen?" Noah asked.

"Yeah," said the waitress. "Why? You got a complaint?"

Noah shook his head. "You done good, Shirley. I'm leaving now. Wrap up the food to go. The kids here will wait for it." He embraced Mike, who squirmed out of his grasp. Then he swung around to me and planted a kiss on my forehead. "Don't let him drive over eighty, Vivi. He only got his license in September." Noah turned away, smoothed back his hair, and walked away toward the kitchen. Mike eyeballed the female under the hat, who was hiding her face behind a menu.

"Who is she?" I asked.

He picked up his napkin and tore it in half. "Friend of Uncle Noah's. Rosita."

"Wonderful!" I glared. "Now maybe you can tell me why she was following me and Gram and what she was doing in Erica's room at the hospital."

His eyes darkened. "I'm not sure. But I'm going to find out. That's the reason I wanted to come here in the first place. I knew I'd find them all in the Scalawag Shack. You with me? You need to make up your mind."

I looked from Mike to the woman with the hat and then turned toward the door. Someone was swinging through it. A man with a beard almost as black as his long billowing coat.

How could I leave when the gang was all here? Rosita put down her menu, took out a mirror, and did things to her lipstick. The Hasid sat down three booths behind her and played peek-a-boo using his *Herald* for a shield. Mike tore his napkin into smaller and smaller shreds, and I tried to keep from having to go to the bathroom.

But nature won out. I excused myself and Mike was on his feet, never leaving my side till we reached the restroom. "I'll wait here, outside the door," he said.

Humongous mirrors took up two walls of the powder room, reflecting the pink padded benches in front of them. The other wall held a changing table and a bin of plastic diaper bags. There weren't any windows in case I needed to escape. I pushed on into the more functional section.

The air in the pink-tiled two-boother was pure disinfectant, pushed around by a tired fan. There wasn't a single window here either. No one could dawdle in this place long and survive. Not even the fly on the ceiling, whose frantic buzz harmonized with the whizz of the fan. Above the sound of the toilet flushing, I heard a *click, click, click.* I held my breath. *Click, click, click.*

I checked the lock, collapsed back on the candy pink toilet seat, and drew my feet up in front of me. It didn't fool anyone! Two high-heeled Bruno Magli slingbacks moved into the open space below my door.

"Ms. Hartman are you in there?" The accent was Cuban with a thick coating of Hebrew.

This was it! O God, I pleaded, staring at the lock, I'll swap you a prayer for a plan. The lock looked so fragile it would give with one good push. Just one good push with her shoulder and she'd have me.

Then I remembered something. It wouldn't have to be that way at all. The door opened out, not in. Careful, Vivi, I told myself, as if I'd ever been anything else. Very slowly I centered myself on the seat and lowered my feet to the floor. She had to believe I was there to stay a while.

The five minutes I waited seemed like forever. Slow as thick syrup I slid the lock back, without making a sound. Then I took a deep breath, rammed the door into her, and bolted out of the room into Mike's unprepared, limp arms.

"Well, hello," he said, recovering his balance. "You were in there a long time. You and Rosita making girl talk?" I was feeling much too weak to hit him.

Mike took my arm. "C'mon back to the table. The waitress brought us some tea to drink while we wait. She assured me it's on the house."

Rosita might have been down but she sure wasn't out. We'd barely got back to the table when I saw her slink to her booth, the big straw hat crowning her ebony head. Not one hair or even a hat pin was out of place. I sipped my tea and looked at the Hasid, three booths behind her. He'd laid down his paper and removed his coat, but he still wore the fur-trimmed hat. From where I sat, it looked as though he'd traded his *Herald* for the pastrami on rye.

"Pastrami!" I dug my nails into Mike's hand. "No Hasid would eat pastrami in a place like this!"

Mike stared at the bearded man. "He's not one of Noah's guys. That's for sure. I wonder if he's the reason my uncle took off."

"You think Noah was trying to lose him?"

Mike shrugged. "All I know is that when we came in, Rosita was still outside. She could have spotted the Hasid and sent the note to warn Uncle Noah."

"You think that a phony Hasid is out to harm your uncle?"

118

"I wouldn't be surprised."

"But why?"

Mike lowered his voice and leaned toward me. "What would you say if I told you my uncle's Mossad?"

I grasped the edge of the table. "Israeli intelligence?"

Mike nodded. "I think they're after a spy from the *St. Louis*."

"You have to be kidding!"

Mike sat up. "Okay. Forget it. I never said a word."

"Well, you don't have to be angry. It is a bit bizarre, you know."

"Yeah, I know," he sighed. "So was the airline ticket he sent me, along with that stupid T-shirt with the red bird on the back. I was supposed to wear it on the way down, his note said." Mike sighed. "I guess that's how the Englishman knew me."

"The one who threw you down at the airport?"

"Yeah. And told me to buzz off. That I really shouldn't be involved at all."

"Involved? Involved in what?" I swallowed a gulp of lukewarm tea.

"Who knows? All my uncle's note said was that my seating had been arranged. I'd be sitting near some girl, a relation of a friend. Her life might be in danger and he was counting on me."

My brain felt muddled. I strained to form the

words. "Danger? Girl? Are you saying he meant me?"

"Shush! Not so loud!" Mike looked around. "Why else do you think I dumped your dinner? How could I know it wasn't poisoned?"

I felt myself falling, tumbling around and around like a piece of corn in one of those hot-air poppers. Then everything went black. There were sounds like pots and pans being banged around and Mike's voice saying my name over and over.

Someone slapped my face. "Wake up! She's still half out of this world. I told you we didn't need the tea. I could have handled her." The accent was Spanish.

A glass grazed my lips. I opened my eyes, resting them on the sandy-haired giant whose mouth moved above his square chin. "Had a spot of sleep, eh wot? Well, never mind, love. Drink this. It will wake you. You'll do very well."

"Perhaps," Rosita said to him. "Perhaps not. But in the end it will be your decision."

The Englishman smiled. "No," he said. "You know very well that we can't involve outsiders. The decision will be hers."

14

They took me out through the kitchen and put me into an open convertible. The tall man got behind the wheel. "No more bike rides for you today, love. You're in no condition for that."

Today? I looked at the clock on the dashboard. Two A.M. I closed my eyes and breathed the cool salt air.

"Feeling any better, love?"

I nodded.

"Good. Your grandma's stable, too. I checked just before we left. Her condition hadn't deteriorated."

"No thanks to you," I said. "Going off and leaving her like that."

"I left her in excellent hands. There isn't a better

nurse around than Sister Jean."

"Maybe. I can't be sure of anyone anymore. What do they call you? Evan? Rocky? You're not a nurse any more than a waiter or tourist. I suppose you're one of 'them' too."

"Rocky is fine, love, and that I am. Sister Jean as well. So you see, she'll take good care of your granny."

"A nun in the Mossad?"

The Englishman laughed. "No, love, she's just one of the group. Missed her in the painting, did you?"

The painting! I caught my breath. I'd forgot all about the painting and poor Pedro. Should I tell this person what had happened back at the apartment? I didn't even know him, but Mike had entrusted me to him. Oh, God—I had to trust Mike or I'd go completely out of my mind!

The breeze picked up and I covered my ears with my hands.

"Shall I put the top up?"

"Please, no." The Englishman braked for a light. I studied his face—the high forehead, the long straight nose, the almost rectangular chin. "Someone broke into the apartment," I said. "Whoever it was stole the list—the list of names that was on the back of the painting."

"I know."

That was all? Just "I know"? I stopped talking. I watched the swaying palms, counted the phantom benches along the boardwalk. I heard the giant waves crashing against their pilings, but I wasn't close enough to see them.

He parked in a visitor's space behind Harborfront Hall. The doorman let us in, and I stared at Pedro standing near his elevator. Aside from the big white professional-looking bandage on his forehead, he seemed okay.

Rocky smiled and pointed to the bandage. "A Sister Jean original. Brilliant, eh? We got him to Emergency as soon as Micah told us what had happened."

Mike? Boy, neat trick! Mike must have called for help when I was at Sadie's getting the coffee!

Rocky handed me over to Pedro. "You look after her now, old man. I'm counting on you." Then he pressed my hand. "I'm counting on you, too, love. But whether or not you help us is your decision." Rocky turned and walked away.

It was only after Pedro had let me into Gram's apartment that I realized I hadn't eaten yet. I had just opened the refrigerator when I heard a knock at the door. I looked at the clock. Three-twenty A.M. Did I dare answer?

"Let me in, this hall is freezing," yelled Sadie. "You'd think they'd turn down the air during the night." She wobbled through the door in a long fleecy robe that matched her pink curlers. The lace of her flannel nightgown curled around the edges of her bunny slippers.

"Your doctor friend left?" she said, looking around. "Good for you. Even for a doctor a girl shouldn't go too far. Play hard to get. Know what I mean?" I knew what she meant. But I didn't know what she was doing there. Not until she walked into the blue room and bounced down on the bed. "I guess it will have to do," she said. "Pedro insists you shouldn't spend the night alone."

In a way I wasn't sorry. Even having Sadie over was better than being all by myself. I was actually glad she was there. But not in the blue room.

I took Sadie's arm. "Come with me. Gram's bed is much more comfortable. It's king-sized." By the time I was in my PJ's she was snoring.

The lamp in the blue room wasn't the greatest, and my eyes were already tired. I almost changed my mind about reading the letters. But something about them, maybe the way they were wrapped in that man's handkerchief, told me they had to be important. The initals "P.O." in the corner of each envelope told me something too. They stood for Patrick O'Riley. I held the letters in a sweaty palm. Did I have the right to open them? Look at the things in my trunk, Erica had told me. Had she meant these letters as well?

With shaking fingers I undid the handkerchief. A couple of loose snapshots fell out. The first was of two little girls, maybe ten or eleven years old, sharing a swing. I turned it over. "Erica and Tessie," the writing said, "April 1939." The other pictured a boy and a girl on a sled at the top of a snowy hill. Her dark eyes shone bright. His fair cheek pressed against hers. There was no writing on the back. There didn't have to be. I knew who they were.

I shuffled through the letters looking for more pictures and came up with a studio photograph. The boy was older, wearing a cap and gown. His mouth was turned into one of those little half smiles that doesn't know whether to laugh or cry. "I Love You," he'd written, and signed it "Pat." There was only one other photograph. It was of a woman—beautiful, with dark hair piled high on her head. Her forehead was smooth above her almond-shaped eyes. Beside her was a teenage boy with a squared-off chin. And behind them both stood Patrick, in a dark suit with a round white collar. His right hand rested on the elbow of the woman, his left on the shoulder of the boy. The caption was in Hebrew. "Jerusalem, 1949. 16th birthday of Marc Steinhardt."

I stared at the boy then ran to the dresser and looked at the photo of Erica and her brother in the old-fashioned frame. I heard Rocky's voice. "I'm counting on you, love." I saw his square jaw moving as he spoke. In German, "Steinhardt" means "hard as a stone." A stone is a rock, isn't it? Even when playing waiter he'd taken the name for stone, the Hebrew word, "Evan." Rocky and Marc Steinhardt had to be the same person. Nothing could stop me from reading the letters now.

Miss Erica Steinhardt
P.O. Box 141
Jerusalem, Palestine

November 2, 1946

My dearest Erica,
Now that the war has ended I can finally tell you I'm in France. The army has me working with displaced war orphans. And now for the real news. I've found Marc. He was right here in Paris through the war. With God's help, he'll be with you soon.

All my love,
Pat

Under the signature he'd drawn a little red bird.

All of the letters were in Hebrew. Most were short, a few were longer. They talked of friends who'd died in the war, or been wounded, or been found in prisoner exchanges. They shared family gossip: *My baby sister, Jean, has entered the convent. She's interested in nursing. I can hardly believe she's already sixteen.* Each letter was sent to the same P.O. Box in Jerusalem.

November 30, 1947

My dearest Erica,
What stunning news! I can hardly believe it. Land for the Arabs. Land for the Jews. You now

have a country of your own. Israel is the perfect name. How wise the United Nations are to have divided Palestine between you.

All my love,
Pat

P.S. A British priest I know is heading for Jerusalem. He was a speech teacher here in France. I told him about the boy's problem. He'll be glad to help and will be in touch with you.

December 22, 1948

Dear, dear Erica,

If I ever hoped for anything for Christmas, it was that the Arabs would be as happy with the land division as the Jews. But alas, they want all of Palestine. I pray for your safety. There's so much I want to say, but I know you too well to think you will ever listen to words of caution. God be with you, my dear soldier, and take good care of Marc. If the going gets too rough, leave him with my British friend.

All my love,
Pat

August 1, 1949

My dear Erica,

Thank God the war is over. You're safe and your country is secure. Of course I'll be there for Marc's birthday. I'll certainly be discharged from the service by then. I miss you both so much that I've

*asked to be posted to Jerusalem. My British friend
tells me they need teachers in the churches there.
With his help, and the help of the Lord, I'll soon be
joining you.*

*Love,
Pat*

September 19, 1949

Dear Erica,

*Couldn't wait to tell you my news. Yes, it's true.
I'll be there by the first of the month. Have to brush
up on my mathematics since I'll be teaching that as
well as anything else they throw at me. The school's
a good one, I hear—St. Anthony's. And speaking of
school, I'm glad Marc is studying hard. My friend
tells me he's got him speaking English with a British
accent thicker than his own. Won't that be wild
when he speaks at the trial of the war criminals? Is
he still determined to tell what he saw on the* St.
Louis? *Take good care of him, Erica dear. They still
haven't caught that Nazi. Who knows what the
maniac might try. See you next month in Jerusalem.*

*Love,
Pat*

My eyes were burning. I longed to close them, to
jump into bed. But there was just one envelope left.
I opened it and a newspaper clipping fell out. It was
in Hebrew: TERRORISTS DESTROY CATHOLIC
CHURCH SCHOOL.

I felt my blood drain. My hands shook so much I could hardly hold the paper. "Jerusalem, November 21. An early morning explosion blasted the schoolroom of St. Anthony's Cathedral killing a priest, Father Patrick O'Riley, and nine of his students." The list zigzagged and blurred before my eyes as I scanned through to the S's: "Saunders, Michael, age 14; Shipley, James P., age 12; Steinhardt, Marcus, age 16."

I don't know how long I sat there staring at the paper. When I looked up next, a haze was fighting the darkness outside the window. Morning was on its way. There was no doubt that Patrick was dead. But what had Marc Steinhardt been doing in a Catholic school? And if Marc was dead, who in God's name was Rocky?

15

Sadie flapped two poached eggs onto my toast like a hash slinger in a fast-food joint.

"You're some sleeper," she said. "It's nearly ten o'clock."

I looked at the sun shining through the kitchen window. "Who, me?"

Sadie sat down with a cup of coffee. "Someone young like you can sleep through a hurricane. Not like me. I didn't sleep a wink. Lay in bed awake all night. And forget about this morning. First the telephone rang. I hoped it would stop but it didn't. Must have rung ten times before I picked up, but you were out like a lox."

"Who was it?"

"The rabbi."

"Dad? Thank God. Did he leave a number?"

Sadie sipped some coffee. "I told him you were still sleeping, that you were out late last night with a nice Jewish boy. Why shouldn't I make him feel good? From what I hear, he's had plenty of trouble in his life."

"But did he leave you a number where I can call him?"

Sadie sighed. "He said I should let you sleep and asked for your grandma." She looked at me then stared down at her cup. "I told him she was out, that I was staying with you till she got back. Was it my place to tell him where she really is, that he should worry when he's so far away? Besides, I wasn't lying."

I pushed my plate away. "But did he—"

"Oh, and he said to tell you the dog's okay. He put him in a kennel where the people speak Hebrew. Such a fuss about an animal you'd think it was a person."

I grabbed her arm. "Please, Sadie, did my father leave a telephone number?"

Her brow furrowed. She looked at me. "Oh yeah. The rabbi wants you to call him. You should do it right away, he shouldn't have to worry about you too. Here's the address and phone number where he'll be." She dug in the pocket of her apron and handed me a grimy piece of paper. "I wasn't even finished writing it all down," she said, "when the

131

doorbell rang and that lady cop handed me the package. Such a nice looking girl doing dangerous work like that. And in high heels yet! If she wants to deliver packages, she can't get a job in the post office?"

"Lady cop? Package?" I pushed back my chair.

"Yeah." Sadie pointed to the counter. "She said it was for you."

I tore out of my seat and flew across the room. Grabbing the long narrow box, I picked up a knife, ripped through the tape, and stared. So Rosita had had Gram's umbrella! She must have come to the hospital dressed in the phony cop's outfit.

"Some people have all the luck," Sadie said. "The police never found my umbrella. It was my husband's, he should rest in peace."

I headed for the bathroom, the most private place I knew. "I'm going to take a shower," I said.

"An umbrella in the shower?" Sadie called after me. "What is that, a new style?"

I locked the door, ran the faucet hard to make things sound kosher, and looked at the umbrella. The "lady cop" had to have been Rosita. But what did she want me to do with this thing? Look for some microfilm a spy had put there fifty years ago? The Mossad could have done that themselves. Still, it wouldn't hurt to look, would it? I pressed the button on the stick and the umbrella flew open like a parachute.

"They hid them in hollowed-out sticks," Mike

132

had said. I moved my fingers along the stick to the joint and twisted. Nothing turned except my sweaty hands, slipping around the metal. I grabbed a washcloth, wrapped it around the stick, and tried to twist it again. It worked. I held my breath.

The long silver tube got longer and longer. The two ends came apart. I held one part to my eye, trying not to shut out all the light. It looked empty. I put down the tube and looked in the other half. Jackpot! About three inches down, something was blocking the light.

I shook the tube. Nothing! I banged it on the tile floor. The lump didn't budge a millimeter. I studied Gram's things on the vanity and grabbed a nail file. It was perfect. A couple of seconds of prodding around the edges, another good shake, and the lump slid into my hand. My God! This wasn't microfilm. It was a bullet!

I rolled the bullet around in my hand. Ouch! It scratched my finger. I examined the bullet more closely. It looked like it had been soldered shut at one end. So this was where they hid their secrets. The microfilm must be inside! No way could I get it open. Not now, anyway. I screwed the umbrella back together and turned off the faucet. Just in time. Sadie was knocking at the door.

"You took a year's lease on the bathroom? Or are you coming out to say hello to the company?" she yelled through the keyhole.

Company! Great. Just what I needed! I drew my

robe tighter and dropped the bullet into the pocket. I walked out of the bathroom clutching the umbrella. But I had to pass the kitchen on the way to the den.

"Wait!" Sadie yelled.

I waited.

"You're lucky," she said. "Look who's here."

I looked. The deaf old guy from the roof, decked out in a white cap and visor, was sitting at the table munching a cinnamon danish. Sadie beamed at him.

"Mr. Johnson came to drive you to the hospital. Isn't that nice of him? While he was waiting, I told him to have a cup of coffee."

"Thanks," I said.

Mr. Johnson kept on munching.

"VIVI SAID 'THANK YOU,'" Sadie shouted to him.

The old man stood and tipped his hat. "My pleasure." He pointed to the umbrella. "You're taking that to your grandmother?"

I shivered. Something about the way he said it made me feel like Little Red Riding Hood. I managed to smile.

Back in my room, I thought of what Rocky had said. "I'm counting on you." I remembered Erica's pleading eyes, her voice—"We're so close." Close to what? So now I had the umbrella, but what was I supposed to do with it? They'd left me to figure that out by myself.

I pulled on some jeans and a shirt and sat on the

bed holding my socks. Erica had simply carried the umbrella and got herself mugged. And Gram had done the same. Was I supposed to walk out and get clobbered too? And how did this all connect to a Nazi spy who'd been on the *St. Louis* fifty years ago?

"Don't forget to call your father before you go," Sadie screamed through the door. I looked at the phone. Would Dad know what to do? I pictured the look on his face if I told him. Then I put on my socks and tied my sneakers. Whatever I did, it would have to be my decision.

The first thing I decided to do was pray. After that I knew I'd take the umbrella. But what to do about the bullet? On TV cop shows, women always hid things in their bras. I took off my shirt and wiggled into a Belgian lace monstrosity. One of Mom's great bargains had found a purpose at last. I put my shirt back on, took a deep breath, and stepped out of my room. Thanks to Mr. Johnson, I'd be safe for a little while, anyway.

"My car's over there," Mr. Johnson said, pointing to the far end of the garage. The old man's wheels probably weren't used any more than the others down here, I thought. Most of the cars we passed were covered with dust. The place was like an underground storage bin, as spooky as a tomb. It was so quiet that my steps echoed on the gray concrete as I followed him.

Click. I spun around. The unexpected sound seemed familiar. "What was that?" I said.

Mr. Johnson didn't answer. He probably never heard me. He kept right on going toward his parking space. Suddenly he stopped. He stood still, leaning on the door of a cool blue truck, a brand-new RV camper.

"Here we are," he said. "Now where's my key?" The sound came closer. *Click, click, click.* Rosita? But she was one of the good guys! My heart stopped. Oh, God—she was a double agent!

The clicking grew louder. The deaf old man didn't hear a thing. He raised his key and fitted it into the lock. I covered his back, raised the umbrella, and got ready to strike. If I held her off till he opened the door, we could jump in fast and maybe make a quick getaway.

The old man was taking forever. Hurry, I prayed. At last he turned, took my hand, and, with surprising strength, pushed me onto the seat. Just as he started to close the door I saw her.

"Watch out!" I screamed. It was so loud that even the deaf man heard it. He spun around and crashed against the woman. There was a loud clunk as her gun hit the ground. Seconds later, Rosita lay crumpled beside it. We were safe. Mr. Johnson brushed himself off and turned to me.

"Okay, little lady," he said, reaching for the umbrella. "Shtay right where you are and hand it over!"

16

"Good morning." The greeting was in English but the accent was Spanish. I tried to turn toward Rosita. It wasn't easy, since I was flat on my back with my feet tied together at the ankles and my hands lashed at the wrists behind my head. I could have been a mummy—only mummies don't ache all over.

The shades in the truck had been drawn and it was almost pitch black inside. From up front in the cab, a radio blared so loudly it hurt my ears. The way we were bouncing around I figured we were doing at least eighty. I rolled against the side and groaned.

"Stop complaining, havaree. We're still alive,

aren't we?" the Spanish-tinged voice said. She'd called me "havaree," but she sure wasn't acting like a friend. "It's all your fault we're here," she said. "If it wasn't for your scream back in the garage, we'd be home free. Old Hauptmann never would have heard me there. He's deaf as a stone from listening to his explosives all those years."

"Hauptmann? I thought his name was Johnson."

"Only for now. We knew he'd fall for that wild newspaper story we planted—that he'd want to get his hands on the phony umbrella in that old rusty box. But we couldn't catch him in the act while he was using that teenage gang. With you, we knew he'd have to do the dirty work himself. It wouldn't look kosher for his gang of hoodlums to target another kid like you."

"You knew he was behind the muggings?"

"We knew Hauptmann was. What we didn't know was his current identity. We had to catch him in the act to find out. So now we have him. Or is it the other way around? But I'm not complaining. In the old days he would have used more than a tranquilizer shot to put us out. His methods were a lot more permanent."

"You're talking about bombs? Like the kind he used in St. Anthony's?"

I heard her breathe. "So your grandmama told you about that. I knew we couldn't trust anyone but Mossad."

Behind my head, I clenched my hands. "Gram

didn't tell me anything. She would have died first. She still might die. And I still don't know why."

"Sorry, havaree. You risked your life for us. The least we owe you are some answers. You see, it all goes back to the *St. Louis*. Marc Steinhardt and his parents were on it. He was just a kid—about six years old. Always got up at the crack of dawn. He'd sit in his favorite hiding place looking out at the sea. One morning he saw something—the ship's steward throwing something overboard. A long metal box."

"And in the box was an umbrella with microfilm inside?"

"You got it, havaree. Hauptmann saw him. Chased him for all he was worth, but Marc got away. When he told his parents, they were terrified. They kept him in their sight from then on. And then, of course, so much else happened."

Rosita stopped and swallowed. "After the war, the UN put the Nazis on trial. Old Hauptmann must have been plenty scared. If he were caught and the kid testified against him, he'd be a goner. He had to find Marc Steinhardt and get rid of him."

"So he blew up St. Anthony's school."

"That's right."

"But why would Marc be there? He was Jewish, not Catholic."

"That's another story, havaree. All I can tell you is it wasn't the first time for the kid. Afterward Hauptmann got some Nazi doctor to change his looks. He'd never left fingerprints. And now he thinks since he has the evidence, too, he's safe. Wait till he finds out the microfilm's as phony as his face."

The truck lurched and almost stopped. For a second I didn't dare to breathe. When I did, I felt the bullet drenched in sweat inside my bra.

"But he doesn't have it," I said. "I do." First there was silence. Then Rosita began to laugh ever so softly.

"Oh, damn, you took it out! You know something, havaree, you're some smart kid! You're the reason we're still alive! He must think Noah has the microfilm and he's going to use us for a trade. Hurry. Roll over!"

"What?"

"Roll over. C'mon, be quick about it. I figure it must be about ten P.M. He's not going to leave us alone forever."

I didn't question. I just pushed my weight to one side and rolled.

"Wiggle your fingers," Rosita said. I did. "They work okay?"

"Yes."

"Good! Slide down on your back and lean your head against my feet!" I slid. "A little more. Good. Now grab the heel of my right shoe."

She was crazy. I was sure of it. But how could I object? I was too scared to move my lips. "Hurry! Do as I say, or we'll end up at the bottom of the bay. And that's not in my orders," Rosita said.

I felt for the shoe and touched the four-inch heel. "That's it. Good! Now pay attention. Twist real hard. Do two clicks to the right, one to the left, and then one to the right again."

She was a regular combination lock. I felt like I was back at my gym locker. "Oh, God," I cried, when the heel came off in my hands.

"Shush!" Rosita warned.

"But it fell off!" I whispered.

"That's what it's supposed to do. Quick! Turn it upside down and catch what falls out." I turned the heel carefully and caught two things—one felt like a toothpick wrapped in plastic, the other like a flat nail file with tiny bumps along one edge. "Got the blade?" Rosita whispered.

"I think so."

"Okay. Time to saw rope. First my hands."

I was supposed to saw her free with a nail file? If my life hadn't been up for grabs I would have laughed. And what was the toothpick for? Cleaning our teeth so we wouldn't have bad breath when we died?

"Be careful with that needle," Rosita said. "One jab of that tranquilizer will put you to sleep for a week. Uh-oh, we're starting up again. He must be running away from someone. It couldn't be Noah. He's out on one of the boats with some tourists. And Rocky wouldn't get this close so soon."

"Maybe it's the guy with the black coat," I said.

"No, havaree. The way that Hasid's been tailing

141

me he has to be one of Hauptmann's boys. The old man's probably got him at the dock waiting for Noah's boat to come in. Better start sawing. But be careful! That blade's a lot sharper than it seems."

As I started to move, the rope on my hands got stuck on her left heel. Was it hollow too? I wondered. I wondered if Rosita would give me the combination, would ask me to open that one next. Then I wondered what was in it. I wondered if it were poison pills like TV spies always swallow when they're trapped. Oh my God. I couldn't even get a vitamin down without gagging!

"Hurry," Rosita said.

But my hand wouldn't budge. No matter how bad it was I had to know. "Tell me what's in there," I whispered.

She sighed and my body went limp. It was all over.

The Spanish-tinged English sliced the darkness. "Chanel Number Five, havaree. Sometimes it comes in handy. But not with an old fossil like Hauptmann."

I was alive again. I sawed at her ropes, my whole body sweaty with the effort. Her hands were soon free. She worked at her ankle ropes and then on all of mine. "Okay," she said. "Now the lessons begin. You'll have to be ready for Hauptmann. He's sure to come around by midnight with another shot to last us until dawn."

I shivered. "How do you figure that?"

Rosita sighed. "I know the way the old boy thinks. He figures Noah has the microfilm and he'll trade us for it. But Noah won't be back with the night boat till daylight. The old boy has to keep us quiet till then."

Again and again Rosita went over the lessons, making me repeat them a hundred times. It would have been a thousand if the truck hadn't come to a sudden screeching stop. Rosita pushed me down on the floor and crept to the window. She lifted the shade. "We're at Haulover Pier," she said. "It's where Noah's boat is docked. Just a few parked cars around. Must belong to the guys out fishing with Noah. I bet their wives are glad they'll be out till dawn."

"Glad? Why?"

"So they can shop all night at Sandy Beach Mall, right across the bridge. Three days before Christmas it's open from twelve till daylight. They call it the 'Midnight Madness' sale. Wouldn't mind being there myself."

Shopping? There were actually people out there shopping for the holidays? Shopping as if the whole world hadn't gone mad? I thought of my mother in Paris and wondered if she were out shopping too. Was she picking out a present for me? Another dress? A lacy slip I'd never wear?

"You're quiet," Rosita said. "Thinking about something nice?"

"My mother."

"Ah. She likes to shop?"

"Sometimes. Most of the time she works very hard."

"Ah yes, like you."

"Me?"

"Yes. Like you learned your lessons. Still remember them?"

"Yes."

"Okay then. What's the first thing we have to do?"

I thought for a second. "As soon as we hear Hauptmann getting out of the cab, we go back to playing lox on the floor."

"Good! And what do we do when he comes to us?"

"I grab his legs. You shoot him with your tranquilizer needle."

"And if his partner with the black coat comes to help him?"

"We separate. You get him to follow you, and I make tracks for the 'safe house.'"

"You remember where it is?"

"I think so. I've been there before."

"Think?" Rosita's hands were on my shoulders. She was shaking me. "You can't just think! You have to know! Go over it again. Get the directions straight in your head. Now tell me. How do you get inside?"

I closed my eyes and saw the door. "I ring the back doorbell three times. One long. Two short.

When someone answers, I tell them who I am. I will say I need protection."

"And who are you? Tell me quick."

I bit my lip. I hesitated, then let the Hebrew words spill out. "Aviva, daughter of Patrick, son of Benjamin the cardinal. But—"

"No 'buts!' There's no time for 'buts.'" She went to the window again.

"Wait! Please. Tell me why my grandfather was called a cardinal." I heard her drop the shade.

"They were all cardinals. The whole group. When the ship was turned back they took an oath. They swore they would never let it happen again. They called themselves the St. Louis Cardinals and wore those little red birds as a symbol. Everyone thought they were just a bunch of dumb kids with a crush on a baseball team. No one suspected the things they did, the lives they saved during those years."

"They saved lives? But how could they? They were just kids."

Rosita sighed. "Some things make kids grow up fast." Her voice seemed to come from far away. "You know, in a way my parents were lucky. They got into Cuba on the last ship before the *St. Louis.* Only they never got their visas for the U.S."

"You mean they were stuck there?"

"Sort of. They kept on hoping until their money ran out. After that they gave up, I guess. My father had been a dentist in Germany. But in Cuba he couldn't get work. The Jewish agencies sent us money to live. I was born and then my sisters. Then the Japanese bombed Pearl Harbor. Things got better for the Jews. Cuba decided to side with the U.S. My dad opened an office in Havana. When Israel was formed, he thought we could go there, and we saved our money for the trip."

"So you left Cuba a few years later?"

Rosita sighed. "Not a chance. By 1959 Cuba had become Communist. Unfortunately for us, the Communist state needed dentists for their new health plan. The rest of us could go they said, but my father had to stay in Cuba. No way would we leave him. We finally got to Israel in 1974." I could tell by the sound of her voice that Rosita was smiling. "That's where I met Noah, my first day in the special forces."

"You mean the Mossad?"

"Yes."

"And Rocky is in it too, of course. Tell me Rosita, who is he?"

"Our commanding officer."

"I mean who is he really?"

"Shush!" Rosita's finger was on her lips. "The radio. It stopped. Lie still! It's our turn now." She reached across the darkness and took my hand. "Not to worry, havaree. You'll soon be safe again." She dropped my hand and I lay in the dark, taut as a marble statue, listening to the thumping of my heart.

17

"Now!" Rosita commanded. I rushed at Hauptmann and clung to his slippery legs while she got a grip on the needle.

"Damn, I dropped it!" I heard her say, as the massive Hasid crashed into the dark truck.

"Caught yiz red-handed! Give up!"

"Run, Vivi, run!" Rosita's cry was sharp. But how could I leave her alone with both of them?

"Run! That's an order!"

I thought, but not for long. "It's okay, havaree, I have it!" I shouted. The Hasid spun toward me with glaring eyes. His long black coat whipped around him. His hand was on the fur-trimmed hat.

I jumped from the truck and tore through the

soupy gray mist. My sneakers skated on the dew-drenched path between some dense bushes and the highway. My eyes were on the drawbridge a few yards south. I had to make it across that bridge before it opened.

I crashed into the bushes, then crept slowly beneath the foliage. I was the second best runner in my school, but the Hasid was already at the bridge while I was crawling around on my stomach like a baby. He was leaning against the abutment, scanning the bushes. His black coat had come open and his white shirt gleamed in the headlights of the whizzing cars. Would he dare to grab me with all that traffic around?

I jumped out of the bushes. Brakes screeched as I threw myself over the railing. A big black limo crunched to a stop as I tore across the road. The Hasid followed. I circled back, waving at the cars. "Help me! Please help me!" No one even waved back.

Red lights flashed. A gate popped up across the highway. The traffic stopped dead! As the draw-bridge opened, the Hasid blasted toward me. There was no time to pray. With one eye on him and one on the widening crack, I jumped. He turned to his side, flipped over the chasm, and landed just behind me, his coat a billowing black balloon.

I didn't wait to see the whites of his eyes. I ran. Houses flew by—a garden—a driveway! I ducked into the dark passage. It ended in an alley where all the driveways seemed to connect. I tore past garages, whizzed by padlocked sheds. Dripping with sweat, I pushed through the endless night. And then there was light! A sign flashed on—a clock with both hands at twelve. "WELCOME TO SANDY BEACH MALL'S MIDNIGHT MADNESS," it said. Beneath the sign was my escape route—the delivery door to Neiman Marcus.

A hand clutched at the back of my shirt. I sprung free and ran into the store. As I fought my way through the perfumed shoppers, I thanked God for those bargain-hunting nuts storming Bonwits, Saks, and Bloomie's. I might be mauled to death here by some sleek sale stalker, but at least I could hide from the man with the long black coat.

Only I couldn't hang out in shopper's heaven forever. A few blocks down was the safe house. But somewhere outside the Hasid was waiting. I ran through the nearest exit and back into the darkness. I sped through the streets, sure he was lurking around each corner. One Hundred Seventy-First Street, One Hundred Seventieth. Just two blocks more. I pushed ahead and stepped off the curb, twisting my ankle. Ouch!

A sharp pain shot from my ankle to my thigh. I ignored it and hobbled on. One Hundred Sixty-Eighth Street. The pain grew worse. I fought back tears but lost the battle. Through the mist, a light appeared, and a sign: "GOLDSTEIN'S DELI—STRICTLY KOSHER."

Rosita's voice banged in my head—"Don't knock, ring! One long. Two short. Three times." I didn't dare breathe. Where in God's name was the bell? "Not the front door, the back one." The Spanish tones nudged me into the alley. One long. Two short. Three times seemed to take forever. Inside, a dim light came on.

"Who's there?" A voice called out in Hebrew.

"I, Vivi." I answered, the foreign words thick on my tongue.

"Who?"

Pain shot through my ankle. "I'm Aviva, daughter of Patrick."

"Impossible!" The light went out.

"Oh, please! Not Patrick the priest. Patrick the rabbi. Son of Benjamin. Benjamin the cardinal." The lamp flashed on again. "Please let me in. I need protection." The pain licked my calf, my knee. I leaned my ear against the door and heard the muffled voices.

"Is it possible? Possible?"

I felt myself sliding, slipping to the ground. Then there was darkness.

I awoke in a pool of blood. No, not blood. A blood red couch. It was soft, velvety. I felt my chest. The bullet was gone. A woman stroked my cheek. "I took it, havaree." Her tanned face had lines like a finely cracked mirror. Gram? It couldn't be. Gram was—I started to cry.

The woman smoothed my hair. "It's all over,

havaree. All those things you told us about are behind you. Drink this. Get your strength back." She held a cup to my lips. I shook my head. I looked at the faded flowers on the carpet and stared at one of Gram's paintings on the wall.

From the other end of the narrow room, a man in a wheelchair rolled toward the sofa. He searched my face with cool gray eyes, squinting under bushy white brows. "So you're awake?" His massive right hand gripped mine. "Myron Goldstein," he said. "This is my wife, Tamar. How do you feel?"

I clutched his sleeve. "Rosita needs help!"

Myron sighed. "So you've said. We've already been over that, havaree."

"But she's there alone with Hauptmann! And the Hasid! What if he comes back?" Oh, God, didn't anyone care? I swung my legs to the floor.

"Ah, yes, the black coat. You spoke of him, too. I'll tell you something, havaree. At some time or other, every Hasid in Miami has had a corned beef sandwich in Goldstein's. But any Hasid who would even taste the water at the Scalawag has got to be a phony. C'mon, let's tell Noah you're okay."

I tried to stand and fell back onto the sofa. Myron rolled across the room and came back with a pair of crutches. "Here. Try these. You're tall enough for mine. The wireless is in there." He motioned with his head. I picked up the crutches. By the time I'd limped to the room he was at the radio. "Okay, shoot. What do you want to say after we tell him you're alive?"

"I'll say it myself, thank you."

He waved his hand impatiently. "Sorry. You'll have to trust me. You don't know the code. It only works in Hebrew—keeps the Coast Guard off Noah's tail." He pushed some keys and signaled me to start. The message tumbled out in one breath.

"Hauptmann in blue truck near dock. Rosita in danger. Hurry! Vivi."

"That's it?"

I bit my lip. The lame man shrugged, hit a few keys, and waited. A tape began to snake out dots and dashes. Myron decoded the words.

"Vivi. Thank God you're okay. Grandmother fine. Woke up last night starving. Noah back at dawn's early light. Love. Mike."

Gram was okay! Thank God. But not one word about Rosita. I sighed.

Myron shook his head. "Still worried about the Cuban bombshell? Listen, havaree, would it help if I told you you did good?"

"What do you mean?"

"You left the agent with one instead of two, didn't you?"

"Big deal."

"Okay, so maybe it wasn't such a big deal. But Rosita doesn't need our help, havaree. Don't you see? She had to get you to safety first and then let Hauptmann take her hostage. She's a professional. Those were her orders. Now sit down and taste this pea soup. The Scalawag's been dying to steal the recipe." Myron looked at his old-fashioned silver pocket watch. "Dawn's early light. Well, Hauptmann always did like early morning best. No one around to cramp his style. No. No one but little Marcus Steinhardt." He laughed.

"You're not eating," Tamar said. She handed me a piece of buttered bread. "You're sure not like your grandma. Only Tessie would wake up from a coma hungry. As a girl I used to envy the way she could eat and eat and never put on a pound."

"That was all right for skinny Benjy Hartman," Myron said. "As for me, I like some flesh on a woman." He pinched his wife's arm playfully. "But still, Tessie did good. Damn good. They all did."

"They?" said Tamar. "And what about you?" She looked at me. "Know how he got his leg blown off?"

I shook my head.

"It was 1948. The UN divided Palestine between the Arabs and the Jews. The Jews were so happy. They named their part Israel."

I sighed. "I know all that already. The Arabs got mad. They declared war. But what has all that got to do with Myron's leg?"

"Plenty," said Tamar. "The Arabs cut off all the roads to Jerusalem. Our people were stranded. Except for Myron's deliveries of food and—"

"Tamar!" The warning was razor sharp.

Tamar looked down at her hands.

"Food and *what?*" I insisted.

Myron waved his hand. "Nothing. Parts of things that no one else in the world wanted. Junk that would still be garbage, if not for Seymour Abramson."

"Abramson?" I jumped. "Any relation to Mike?"

Myron shrugged. "Guess you might as well know everything. He's Micah's father. Our engineer. A regular alchemist, that one. Turned trash into weapons in that dark little basement in the Bronx."

"The Bronx? But how did you get it to Israel?"

Myron smiled. "Good old Noah found us an ark. An old Navy tub. It was so loaded down only God could keep it afloat."

"But he didn't have to make it that light, did he?" Tamar laughed. She looked at me. "It tossed on the waves like a bathtub toy. Oy, were we seasick volunteers. Your granddad had his hands full treating us. And he wasn't even a doctor yet."

"Grandpa was there too?"

"Of course. As soon as we got there, Benjy, Tamar, and Jeanie went to work in the hospital. The others joined the army, and I was put in charge of delivery." Myron shrugged. "One night the Arabs ambushed my truck."

Tamar turned to me. "You know why he got to do the deliveries? Because he was always a businessman. Even as a kid."

I thought about Erica's diary. About the raffle Myron had started to help Erica get to Cuba. "I

154

know," I said.

Myron looked at me, his brow furrowed. Tamar turned to her husband and smiled. "We were quite a team, weren't we? Even in school, back when it all started."

"Sure," said Myron. "The real St. Louis Cardinals wouldn't know from it. Skinny Benjy Hartman already acting like a bloody doctor, pricking each of our fingers for the vow." Myron put his hand over his heart and closed his eyes as he spoke.

We shall never forget the St. Louis
We shall fight for a homeland for the Jews
Though our blood spills red as the cardinal
Red birds do not fly away.

"What times those were." Tamar sighed. "The worst and the best, as they say. Your grandma was a great artist in those days."

"She's still pretty good."

They both laughed. "But not with passports," Myron said. "Bet she hasn't done one in years."

"Passports?"

"That's right. We used to collect them from everyone we knew. Then Tessie would fix them up a little. After that, we'd get them to Patrick to use for his kids."

I stared at him.

"The first one was the hardest," Tamar said. "Going against the law didn't agree with Tessie's conscience. But how could she refuse to help save Erica's little brother, Marc?"

"Wait a minute!" I held up my hand. "I thought Patrick brought Marc to Israel."

Myron sighed. "Sure, eventually. But it wasn't all that easy. For starters, he had to find him. The captain of the *St. Louis* had helped the Steinhardts get to Paris. But the Nazis soon took over France, too. It didn't take them long to start rounding up the Jews and shipping them off to concentration camps. The day the Gestapo came looking, old man Steinhardt hid Marc in a closet, inside a bundle of laundry. He put a gag in the kid's mouth to keep him from screaming for his mama and prayed some kind person would find him."

"Poor little tyke," Tamar said. "The landlady discovered him a day later and took him to church. The fathers kept him safe until the war in Europe was over. That's where Patrick finally caught up with him."

"Pat was an army chaplain then," Myron continued. "He was in charge of orphaned kids in Europe. He longed to get Marc united with Erica. But the Jews didn't have a country yet. Erica was in Palestine. And Palestine was controlled by the British who weren't letting any more Jews in."

"So he used one of Gram's phony passports?"

Myron nodded. "You got it, baby. On the passport Marc was a Christian, English kid."

Tamar laughed and slapped her knees. "Tessie and Patrick! What a team! It worked so well they got hundreds of kids through."

I thought about Gram. Yes. About her I could almost believe it. "But a priest breaking the law?" I said aloud.

Myron's answer was ready, like he'd used it many times before. "For Patrick, there was no choice. In times like those most people asked, 'Where is God?' But Pat never questioned the guy upstairs. He asked, 'Where is man?'"

"He worried about everyone," said Tamar. "But mostly he worried about Marc."

"But I thought Marc was safe in Israel."

"In Israel, yes. Safe, no! The Allies were holding trials in Germany for Nazi war criminals. They needed witnesses from the *St. Louis* and Marc agreed to be one. Hauptmann must have panicked. If he were ever captured, and if Marc Steinhardt lived to testify, Hauptmann's life wouldn't be worth two cents. Things began to happen."

"What kinds of things?"

Myron and Tamar exchanged glances. "Oh, a bullet just missing Marc's head as he walked home from school," Tamar said. "A bomb planted in his bicycle pack, which by some miracle was a dud. And other gems like that."

"But why would Hauptmann blow up a church school?"

Myron reached for an apple and polished it on his sleeve. "To eliminate Patrick, of course, so he could get to the kid. Pat was Marc's guardian, and he was worried about all the goings-on. He left the

157

army and took a teaching job in Israel. He stuck to that boy like a shadow. A tall black penumbra with a white collar."

"And he made him go to a Catholic school?"

"No! Of course not!" Tamar shouted. "Don't you see? Adding Marc's name to the list was his final act of love for the child."

I looked from Myron's face to Tamar's, uncomprehending.

Myron slammed down the apple. "Look, the bomb strikes, okay? Pat's hit. He knows he's dying. How will he protect Marc now? There's only one way. He's got to make Hauptmann think that the kid died, too." Myron leaned back in his wheelchair, a sad smile on his lips. "You know something? It worked. That damn Nazi never hounded Marc again."

"And now it's Marc's turn," said Tamar. "Now Marc—alias Evan or Rocky Steinhardt—is determined to end Hauptmann's treachery once and for all."

I thought about the dead kids stretched out on the floor of the schoolroom, their schoolbooks and papers on fire. I thought about the priest groping for his pen, his bloody body creeping toward the roster. I remembered the words from "Ethics": "To save one life is like saving the whole universe." And I was glad my Dad had been named for Patrick.

"Well, what do we do now?" I asked.

"I'm going to make tea," said Tamar.

Myron smiled. "You see? The decision has been made. Until dawn's early light, we'll sit right here and sip tea."

I looked at him. "That's all?"

He smiled. "Well—maybe, after that, we'll go watch the action from the ramparts."

18

Our rampart was a grassy hill overlooking the bay. The water below us glistened. It rippled like sapphire Jell-O against the side of Noah's Ark. Bouncing against the dock, the boat looked like a whitewashed sentinel, its crest a blue six-pointed star.

A fat-bellied pelican surveyed the boat with its beady black eyes, then went back to prodding a small dead fish with its beak. It was an orange beak, the color of my mother's favorite lipstick. Aside from that, the pelican didn't resemble my mother at all. My mother's eyes weren't black but brown like mine. She wasn't fat but tall and slim like me. Maybe I was like my mother, I thought—

more than I'd ever wanted to admit.

"It's begun," Myron whispered. "Here they come." A man walked out on the deck of the boat. I could tell by his walk it was Noah. "Here come Hauptmann and Rosita," Tamar said, looking through a pair of black field glasses.

I shaded my eyes. "I don't see anyone. Where?"

"Down the dock, near the fish-cleaning shed. Here, try these." I squinted into the field glasses and saw Rosita walking slowly toward the boat. Hauptmann was prodding her back with something that might have been a gun. He looked as if he were talking.

"What is he saying? Can anyone hear what he's saying?"

"Shush," Myron warned. He grabbed the glasses. "Noah's turn. I can't hear that either." He handed back the glasses in time for me to see Rosita whirl. Her leg shot out in a high, swift kick. Hauptmann dropped the gun. He covered his face and crumpled to the pavement. Rosita limped toward the boat.

"He's down. He's down," I shouted, "but something's wrong with Rosita. She's hurt."

Tamar reached for her glasses. "Looks like she broke her leg. Uh-oh, Hauptmann's up again. Get him, Noah!"

"What's young Micah doing there with that dog?" Myron asked.

I grabbed the glasses again.

Noah drove a left to Hauptmann's mouth. The

Nazi kicked him in the shin. Then my eyes turned to Mike on the other side of the cabin. He had Noah's dog by the collar. Bearing down on Mike and the dog was the phony Hasid in the fur-trimmed hat. His pistol was drawn. His long black coat billowed like a kite behind him.

Get him, dog, get him, I prayed. Mike bent over the dog, his hand waving toward the Hasid. The dog lay down and turned over. Mike tried again. The dog sat up and begged. The Hasid raised his gun. He flew toward Mike, tore past him, and lunged at lame Rosita.

I stopped praying and started running. Forgetting the pain in my leg, I flew over the hill. *"Kelly k'chee et ha kovah!* (Kelly, get the hat!)" I screamed in Hebrew. The dog leaped to attention. *"Achshaav!* (Now!)" I shouted. He took off and leaped at the man in black.

After it was over, I sat with the others on deck. Hauptmann was tied in one chair, the Hasid in another. Rosita relaxed in a lounge with a "Tamar Special" emergency splint on her leg.

"How did you get that dog to move?" Mike asked me.

"Pilpul," I said. "One, I'd seen you chase him at the airport. The more you yelled, the more he ran away. Two, I could tell the hound was trying, but he got your orders all mixed up. I figured he probably didn't know English. And that naturally led me

to three—he's Noah's dog and Noah's home is
Israel. Since the dog lives there most of the time, his
language has to be Hebrew."

"Uh-uh, not good enough," Mike shook his
head. "It doesn't explain how you knew his name."

"You're right. I have to confess. On that one I
played the odds. *Kelev* means dog in Hebrew. Practically every dog I'd ever met in Israel was named
Kelly."

"Listen, you idiots," the Hasid said. "Stop your
yakking and get these things off me! I showed you
my badge, didn't I? I'm Sammy Greenberg, FBI,
Narcotics." He nodded toward Hauptmann. "The
pusher here is mine. He's been hiring kids to do
muggings, paying them off with drugs. I got enough
against him to put him away for ten years. Okay, so
I made a little mistake thinking the woman and
these kids were with him. But they sure acted suspi-
cious." He stopped and pointed to me. "And when
this girl yelled that *she* had it, I thought she was
running with the evidence."

Noah laughed. "You were right, Hasid. Vivi did
have the evidence. But not yours, ours. Our Israeli
ambassador in Washington is meeting with the
State Department right now. Our Mossad comman-
der will soon have some news. If you're kosher,
you'll go free. But as for the Nazi over there, ten
years is a picnic compared to what's waiting for
him back in Israel."

From somewhere inside the cabin, a wireless

started to click. And a few minutes later a man appeared on deck. He stooped to make it out of the cabin, his blue eyes squinting against the sun. Gray streaks feathered his fair hair. There were deep creases in his forehead. I knew by the square jaw he was Marc Steinhardt.

"Hauptmann belongs to Uncle Sam, but only for now," he said. "Jerusalem settled for U.S. custody with guaranteed deportation to Israel. Turn him over to Greenberg. He's kosher—FBI."

"FBI, maybe," said Myron, "but kosher, no. Next time you play Hasid, Greenberg, don't get caught noshing at the Scalawag. The outfit goes better with Goldstein's kind of food."

It was still early when I left them. I couldn't wait to visit Gram. From the hallway, I saw her propped up in bed. She was talking to Erica, who sat in a wheelchair beside her. As I entered the room they pulled apart sharply.

"She heard," Erica said.

"How much did you hear?" my grandmother asked.

"Not a thing," I answered, kissing first one then the other. "Don't tell me there's something I'm not supposed to know."

"No—I mean, yes," said Gram. She looked at her friend. "Oh, Erica, why don't we tell her now. After all, it *is* Hanukkah."

"Yes, it is." Erica smiled at me. "You know, Vivi, the painting called *The Meeting* is really mine.

Everyone posed so Tessie could paint it for me. It helped me through some very bad times. I wanted it hung to help us through again. And it did."

"And now we want you to have it," said Gram.

"Me?" I said, gaping at each woman in turn. "How come?"

Gram held out her arms. "Because, my darling, it's Hanukkah, and you are one of the group."

Mike and I were together a lot in the next few days: lying on the beach, goofing around on the bike, going to Goldstein's for kosher spaghetti and meatballs. One day I fixed us a lunch in Gram's apartment. From the kitchen, I could see him staring at *The Meeting*, his giant horned-rimmed glasses leaning toward the painting. "There they are," he said suddenly, pointing to two kids in the circle. "There are my mom and dad!" I was standing beside him now and his voice dropped. "You know, I always wondered why they'd never tell me much about growing up in the Bronx. I guess I kind of knew they'd broken the law. My own parents. So old now. It's hard to believe."

That's when I told Mike what my father had told me. I'd called Dad the morning after everything at the pier. Dad had spent five minutes making sure I was alive. Then, since I was, he spent ten more ranting about the risks I'd run. When I asked him whether he'd known about Grandpa and Gram, his tone turned real pulpity. "Of course I knew what they'd done, Vivi," he said. "But how could I let you in on it? What would you have thought of your grandparents? You were still a child, and children think in black-and-white. They never see shades of gray."

Mike's forehead puckered. "What's that supposed to mean?"

I shrugged. "Who knows? Dad talks like that a lot. You might as well know—he's a rabbi."

On the last night of Hanukkah, Noah hosted a party on his boat. Rosita came with a cast on one foot and a flat-heeled shoe on the other. I wore my orange synthetic silk dress, and Myron and Tamar brought enough food for an army. Gram was there, and Erica, and even the FBI. We sailed out into the harbor and lit all eight candles of the menorah.

I was stuffing my mouth with a luscious potato pancake when Marc ran up to me waving a wireless message. "It's from your mother, love," he said. "From France."

I tore the paper out of his hands, my heart beating a hard rock tempo. I ducked into an alcove where I could be alone. I stared at the big black letters.

"Vivi darling. Heard all about it from Gram. You're my kind of a girl!"

"Yes, Mom," I whispered, "I guess I am." A cool breeze was blowing off the bay, but I felt warm all over.

Mike came along, put his arm around me, and drew me to the railing. "This isn't 'goodbye,'" he said. "Toronto and Buffalo are only two hours apart." The strains of "Rock of Ages," drifted toward us, but we didn't join in the singing. I stood looking out at the bay where the *St. Louis* had been forced to turn back, and a wailing cry mingled with the words of the song.

"Do you think it will ever happen?" I asked.

"What?"

"You know, like the song says, 'And we'll see, all men free, tyrants disappearing.' Do you think the world will ever be that way?"

Oh, how I wanted him to say, "Yes." To press my hand and answer, "Of course it will, havaree." But I guess Mike didn't have the answer either. He pressed my hand but he didn't say anything.

Historical Note

On May 13, 1939, the luxury liner *St. Louis* set sail from Hamburg, Germany. Its destination was Havana, Cuba. Its passengers were Jewish refugees.

After being denied entrance to Cuba and the United States, the ship sailed back to Europe, where the passengers were allowed to disembark in Belgium, the Netherlands, France, and England.

By the end of World War II, Nazis had murdered six million European Jews in concentration camps. It is not known how many of the *St. Louis* passengers survived the war. One estimate is that of the 907 passengers who were forced to return to Europe, only 240 lived. The rest were part of Hitler's "final solution."

Author's Note

It was in 1938, in the Bronx, that I first saw Erica. She was clutching her uncle's hand as he brought her to where we kids were jumping rope. "She's a refugee," he said, "ten years old. You kids play nice with her, yes?" He broke free of the little girl's grasp, said something to her in German, and walked back to his candy store on the corner.

I dropped my end of the jump rope and stared. I'd heard about refugees on the radio. I'd seen some in the newsreels at the movies. But I'd never met a refugee in person. I examined her blue coat with the neat velvet collar and the matching hat. But what impressed me most were her thick brown woolen stockings and high laced leather shoes. Erica pointed to the rope and smiled.

It didn't take long for her to learn our games, our language, and our ways. But, except for the fact that her parents were still in Germany, I learned very little about her.

A year later, my family moved to a different neighborhood, and in 1941 the United States went to war. By the time the war ended, I'd grown up and learned what had happened to the Jews in Europe. The memory of a little girl with thick brown woolen stockings and high laced leather shoes filled my mind and wouldn't go away. I created this fiction about the little girl from Germany after hearing the shocking experiences of other

Holocaust survivors. I am deeply indebted to the following people, for sharing their stories with me:

Chaim Kahn, whose family was killed by the Nazis. On November 9, 1938, the Night of Broken Glass (Kristallnacht), he saw ruthless, club-wielding mobs smash the windows of Jewish shops. He saw an old Jewish man lying in the gutter while some Nazis pulled his beard, spit, and shouted curses at him. Gangs ran through the streets shouting "Judenrein, Judenrein! Germany must be Judenrein (free of Jews)!"

Melvin Davidson, whose parents could get only one visa to enter the United States from Lithuania. "You are eleven years old," his father told him. "You will be the one to go now." When the rest of the visas came through, his parents and the baby would join him. Melvin sailed to America on the British ship *Queen Mary* and lived in his uncle's home. His parents didn't make it to his bar mitzvah or to his high school graduation. Melvin started college, then quit and joined the United States Army. But he was too late to help save his family. They were killed by Lithuanian troops as Nazi armies invaded the country.

Edith Cohen, whose family had arrived in Havana a few months before the ship *St. Louis*. She remembers how she waited impatiently to hug her aunt and uncle and play again with her favorite cousin, Sol. But the *St. Louis* docked way out in the bay and never came into the harbor. Every day Edith and her family went to visit their relatives, rowing out to the ship on a small fishing boat. But the passengers never got off. On the sixth day, the *St. Louis* turned around and left.

"No one will let them in," Edith's father said. He said they were stateless people, and they would go back to Germany and end up in concentration camps.

"But I was only seven," Edith says. "I did not know about concentration camps. I only knew I had lost my playmate again and I cried and cried and cried."

Dr. Sol Messinger, who was seven years old when he was a passenger on the *St. Louis*. He recalls, "I stood on the deck one night with my father, praying the United States would let us in. 'What are those lamps?' I asked, looking at the lights that seemed so close by, on the shore.

"'That's a city in the United States,' my dad answered. 'It's called Miami.'

"I go to Miami often now," Dr. Messinger says. "I stand on the beach, look out upon the water, and see myself and my father on that deck. We were only about a mile away from there, yet for us on the *St. Louis,* Miami was as far away as the moon."

About the Author

Like the members of "the group" in her novel, Harriet K. Feder grew up and attended public school in the Bronx. After working her way through college, she taught social studies for 16 years. But writing was always her first love. After her children were grown, she began to write for other people's children. Feder is a mother of three and grandmother of four. Her books for children have been acclaimed both here and abroad. An instructor with the Institute of Children's Literature in Redding, Connecticut, she lives with her husband, Herbert, in western New York.